The Holly Project

KATE STERRITT

Editing and cover design by Murphy Rae at Indie Solutions
www.murphyrae.net/

Formatting by Polgarus Studios
www.polgarusstudio.com/

Dedication

To my mum. I miss you.

"Keep love in your heart. A life without it is like a sunless garden where the flowers are dead."
- Oscar Wilde

Prologue

Biting my lip, I tried to contain my distress as she thrashed around on the bed, yelling incoherent thoughts. I wanted to be strong for her, but the tears were threatening and I was losing the battle to keep them at bay.

"I'm going to call the ambulance. It's time." With his head hung low, Dad left the room.

I wanted to tell him not to leave me alone with her but instead bit my tongue. And what did he mean? Time for her to die? Time to acknowledge we couldn't do this anymore? Time to admit defeat? For the past few weeks, it had been getting worse. It was like her mind had gone, leaving a frantic stranger in a frail and cancer-ridden body. I feared my own mother - the woman I loved more than anyone in the world, the woman who had loved, protected and raised me.

The tears escaped. "I'm not ready, Mum."

I couldn't reach her anymore, and I worried that she would never listen to me again. And worse, that I would never hear her again. I couldn't even remember her voice.

There's something about the sound of ambulance sirens that

makes you panic. It's the sound of fear. And this time, the sirens were for someone I knew, so the fear had turned into a monstrous beast, taking over my body and threatening to swallow me whole.

Pushing past the lump in my throat, I surprised myself by saying I'd go in the ambulance with Mum. I knew I should be with her. She needed me, and I didn't know how much longer I'd be able to say that.

The back of the ambulance was claustrophobic. Mum was lying on the gurney being hooked up to God knows what. The paramedic was trying his hardest to put an oxygen mask on her face, but she kept batting it away. The more he persisted, the more violent she became. It might have been funny if it wasn't so goddamn horrific.

"She doesn't want it," I said, stating the glaringly obvious. "Can you leave it off, please?" I knew the guy was just trying to do his job, but at this point, I just wanted her to be as peaceful as possible.

Arriving at the hospital, a nurse ushered me into a waiting room. Dad arrived soon after with my younger sisters, April and Jamie. At just eleven and six, they were oblivious to just how grim the situation was.

"How come Holly got to ride in the ambulance?" Jamie whined.

"Shut up!" April shouted. "Just get over it. You haven't stopped whining the whole way here."

Dad tried his best to put on a brave face, but I could see he was about to break. "We'll be able to see your mum soon."

Eventually they allowed us into the tiny, windowless room. I wish they hadn't. It was intimidating, at best. The smell of disinfectant and death made me want to cover my face. Mum was lying on the bed, hooked up to an array of wires and tubes. She was awake, but there was something different about her now. Looking back, I think it was that she had accepted her fate. The fight was over. My fierce, funny, beautiful mum was already gone.

April and Jamie clung to Dad and started to sob. Hugging them protectively to his side, his eyes darted around the room. He looked lost and distressed. He was biting his bottom lip so hard, I was sure he would draw blood. I needed to step up.

Rubbing my palms against my forehead, I moved slowly to Mum's side. I couldn't work out how I was supposed to say goodbye to her forever. I felt like my brain had shut down. I wanted to run away as fast as I could. Instead, I looked her in the eye and started to speak.

"Bye, Mum. I love you. I'm going to miss you so much," I choked. "I promise to make you proud."

Taking hold of her hand, I kissed her cheek. It felt like she squeezed my hand briefly, but that may have been wishful thinking. I glanced back at April and beckoned her over. She took a deep breath, then edged forward. She looked terrified.

"Bye, Mum." She gave her a quick kiss on the cheek, then rushed back to Dad, pale and distraught.

Jamie, crying hysterically, refused to go anywhere near the bed. Why was this happening to us?

I took the girls home, leaving Dad to be alone with Mum. My best friend, Audrey, called as soon as we got home, wanting a full update. She loved my mum and often referred to herself as the fourth Ashton daughter, having practically lived at our house since we were five years old. Audrey was more than a best friend;

she was the sister I got to choose. Having to tell Audrey how sick Mum really was made it all too real. I ended the call quickly before the grief crushed me.

Lying in bed that night, I watched the hours on my bedside clock slowly tick by. The loneliness I felt, coupled with a bubbling anger deep in my gut, was overwhelming. I was too young to deal with this. I wasn't strong enough. I didn't *want* to be strong enough. I was only fourteen. *Fifteen*, I corrected myself as the clock ticked past midnight.

As daylight started to filter through my blinds, I heard Dad's car rumble down the driveway. I dragged myself out of bed and headed to the kitchen.

"Your mother is gone, Holly," whispered my father. I felt my legs give way.

They were the words I had been dreading for months. I was mature for my age – watching your mother deteriorate will do that to a girl – but at that moment, I felt like a naive child, one who'd been hoping for a miracle.

"Her heart gave out early this morning. She couldn't be revived," he choked. "She's not suffering anymore."

I was only half-listening. All I could think about was the last time I'd seen her.

Sitting on the kitchen floor with my face buried in my bent knees, I let the tears fall. I cried for the pain she'd suffered since her cancer returned a year ago. I cried for the enormous hole she was leaving in our family. I cried for the eternal grief my father was going to endure. I cried for April and Jamie, who barely knew her. But most of all, I cried because I was weak and I knew, from then on, I needed to be strong...

Happy birthday to me.

Chapter One

Ten years later

Happy birthday to me.

A quarter of a century? I felt old - *really* old. I heard the front door close. It was early for them to be going to work, but my flatmates, Audrey and Zara, knew to avoid me on my birthday. I had a date with the couch, the TV, a box of tissues and my favourite ice cream. Switching off my emotions usually wasn't a problem – except on this one day of the year, when I allowed myself to open old wounds, feel everything and have my own personal meltdown. It was the one day of the year I grieved my own fate. My mother died of the same disease that claimed her mother, and her grandmother before that. I was a ticking time bomb.

Tomorrow I would go back to pretending to be the strong, independent woman everyone expected me to be.

Pretending.

Stepping out of the shower, my long, dark hair dripping wet, I thought I heard the front door close again.

"Get dressed, Holly," called a familiar male voice through the bathroom door.

"What are you doing here, Jason? Your spare key was only for emergencies." Despite the protection of the closed door, I was shocked by the intrusion and embarrassed by my nakedness.

"It *is* an emergency. You have to come in to work today, and I knew you wouldn't answer your phone. You'll thank me, I promise."

"Absolutely not. Go away!"

Wrapping a towel tightly around my body, I strode out of the bathroom, determined to get him the hell out of my apartment. There was nothing going on between us, but seeing him standing in my living room, his dark suit perfectly tailored to his broad shoulders, made me weak at the knees. And there you have it. I can't be around anyone today. Emotional and needy have no business with me.

"Ready to go then?" he asked, laughing as he looked me up and down.

"Jason, this is my one day. I thought you of all people would understand."

"Holly, I know this is a tough day for you, but it's been ten years. She would want you to take your seat at the adults' table." He stepped forward and hugged me. "Ryan Davenport flew in from London last night. He's asked for the presentation to be brought forward to this afternoon."

I breathed in his aftershave, resisting the urge to bury myself in his chest and hide from the world.

"Can't you stand in for me?" I asked. "I'm sure Slater won't mind. You know my design almost as well as I do."

"If you're not there, Eva will have the upper hand. We were both at the office early this morning when the call came through. She was obviously thrilled you wouldn't be there. I asked Slater if I could come and get you."

Eva "Bitch" McCormack was my arch-rival. She played dirty and was constantly looking for ways to undermine me. We were the two youngest architects at the firm, but our design styles were as different as our appearances and personalities. Her designs were all glitz and glamour, while I always strove for understated elegance and intelligent layout. Eva epitomised every man's fantasy with her model figure, long caramel hair and piercing blue eyes. She wasn't above flaunting her boobs, either, if it got her what she wanted.

Jason and I studied architecture together at the University of Sydney and both managed to secure coveted internships at Slater Jenkins. Eva started her internship at the same time, took an immediate dislike to me and spent all her time flirting with Jason. A few months ago, the three of us were asked to submit a design for the Davenport project. Jason's workload was already unmanageable. He was working with another senior partner on the Hong Kong project, so he had to pass up the opportunity.

I had to make a decision. Wallow in my own pity party or suck it up, face the world and take the opportunity. This was the one day of the year I allowed myself to be weak, but today I had no choice.

Breathe in, breathe out.

By sunset, it would be over for another year - I could do this. One foot in front of the other.

I chose a simple, charcoal grey tunic dress over a white shirt and my favourite black boots. With my hair pulled back into a ponytail, I took a little more care than usual on my makeup. I couldn't help noticing the sadness in my grey-green eyes as I stared at my reflection in the mirror. They were my mum's eyes – doe eyes. Audrey always told me they were exotic and sexy. Today, they reminded me of the vacant stare I'd spent the last ten years trying to forget.

Breathe in, breathe out.

"You know you've ruined me for every other woman, don't you?" moaned Jason as I emerged from my bedroom.

"Thanks, Jase, but you don't have to be nice to me today. I'm totally fine."

"I'm not being nice. I'm being honest." Considering my fragile emotional state, his sincerity was unsettling.

"Let's get this over with," I stated firmly. "Tonight, I'll need wine - a lot of wine."

Chapter Two

One of the many joys of inner-city living was being able to walk to work. Audrey, Zara and I lived in a three-bedroom luxury apartment overlooking Hyde Park on the south-eastern edge of the Sydney CBD. Zara's dad had bought it for her when she graduated from law school. The rent we paid her was a fraction of what the market would have commanded.

Audrey and I met Zara during orientation week at university. Even though she was a disaster with directions, Audrey was confident she knew where we needed to be. The university campus could be very confusing, and we had become completely lost. We stumbled upon Zara, who had been equally disoriented, so the three of us worked out the map together. She was wild and crazy, yet kind and generous. The three of us spent almost all our free time together. Soon after classes started, Jason and I were paired for an assignment, and our trio soon became a tight foursome.

Stepping outside, I was greeted by a gorgeous winter day – my favourite kind. Clear, blue sky with a cold breeze. Perfect skiing weather, I thought to myself. Mum loved to ski. I pulled my coat and scarf tighter around my body, shaking off the thought.

"Are you okay?" Jason asked, seeing my face scrunch up and my palm rubbing my forehead.

"Yep, fine. Just a bit nervous."

He put his arm around my shoulders and pulled me in close.

"I need a coffee," I said, eyeing the café at the bottom of our building.

"Okay. I'll let Slater know you're coming. See you up there."

I tried to convey my gratitude without getting emotional. "Thanks, Jason."

"Love you, Hol."

"No, you don't." He laughed at my standard response as he headed for the revolving doors.

"Hey, gorgeous. The usual?" asked my favourite barista in the whole world.

"What would I do without you?" I paid the exorbitant price for my drug of choice, then found a table by the window and sat down to give myself a small pep talk.

I stared out the window at the passers-by, taking note of the smallest details, trying to imagine what was going on in their lives. I always did this when I needed to relax. It helped me get out of my own head.

Two older guys in tight Lycra bike shorts jogged past and waved. *Ugh.* A slightly dishevelled businessman glanced at his watch repeatedly as he half-walked, half-jogged up the hill. I smiled to myself. *He overslept. He is willing time to slow down. He needs to make it to his desk before his boss comes out of the morning meeting.* By contrast, a woman pushed a double pram slowly past. *In a rare moment when both twins are asleep, she gazes longingly at the office buildings towering around her. She's remembering the glamorous life she had before children and wondering why her world-class mediation skills are no match for her toddlers.* A couple of middle-aged women in ill-fitting suits smiled condescendingly at the mother before shaking their heads and rolling their eyes at each other, clearly irritated by the cumbersome pram. Reluctantly, they moved aside to make way.

Caught up in my people watching, I suddenly became aware of someone standing at my table. Looking up, I drew a sharp intake of breath that I desperately hoped was inaudible.

"Do you mind if I share your table?" he asked, in the sexiest voice I'd ever heard. "All the seats are taken."

Before I had a chance to answer, Darren's voice sang out. "Hotty, skim cap!"

Talk, Holly. Say something – introduce yourself. Stop staring at the hot man and say something intelligent!

My reply came out in a bumbling stammer.

"Um… Hi, I'm Hotty… Oh God… I mean, Holly. It's nice to mate you. I mean, meet you! Oh God… um." I looked to my shoes to break eye contact.

Seriously, Holly. Who are you and what have you done with your brain?

"Hi, Hotty. It's lovely to mate you, too." His smile could make me forget my own name. *Oh wait, already did that.*

"Um, have a seat. I'll just grab my coffee." I was completely flustered by the god-like male standing so close to me. "Sorry about Darren. He always calls me Hotty; he likes to embarrass me."

"I think Darren has the *hots* for you, Holly. Can't say I blame him, either. I'll get your coffee." His eyes swept over me, then back up to meet my eyes, holding my gaze for a moment before heading over to get my coffee. He was mesmerising.

"I'm Ryan, by the way," he said when he returned, coffee in hand.

Given that I was a reasonably tall five-feet-eight, Ryan had to be over six feet. I found him intimidating, yet strangely compelling. Definitely older than me, but it was hard to tell by how much. He was around thirty at a guess. He had short, dark blonde hair and an olive complexion, but it was his eyes that were startling. They were the deepest shade of blue I'd ever seen. Sapphire would be the only colour to do them justice. I felt like I could see straight through his eyes, deep into his soul. *Seriously, did I just think that?* I sounded like a sappy, lovesick puppy. Actually, I sounded like my flatmates. This wasn't good.

Ryan took a seat opposite me and sipped his coffee. He didn't take his eyes off me. "So, what had you so captivated out there?"

"Oh, um, I find people watching relaxing."

He appeared genuinely interested. "Why?"

"I don't know. Perhaps I just like to think about someone else's life for a change," I responded with uncharacteristic candour. "I'm in my bubble and they're in theirs. It's my 'imagine-their-life' game."

"Okay then. Try it on me."

"What do you mean?"

This was completely surreal. I had only just met this man, but we were chatting away like we were friends. For some reason, I felt comfortable around him, despite his intimidating hotness.

"Well, you don't know me, yet, so describe the life you'd assign to me if I just walked past the window."

"Okay, let's see." I stared out the window and imagined Ryan walking by. "You have a good job – maybe something creative. You're a decision-maker. You're on your way to an important meeting."

Ryan shook his head and laughed, clearly amused by my little game. He leant forward. "Go on."

I took a deep breath before continuing.

"Okay. You live with your girlfriend in Mosman. Your right hand is in your pocket clutching a small, blue box. It's a diamond engagement ring you just picked up from Tiffany & Co. You plan to ask her to marry you this weekend. Your parents will be over the moon. They epitomise the happily-married couple, living in their mansion overlooking Balmoral Beach. Your sister, Margot, is a paediatric doctor. She's married to her high-school sweetheart, Joshua, who is also a doctor. He is currently abroad volunteering with Médecins Sans Frontières."

"Oh my God, Holly. You're hilarious," he replied, chuckling. "Is that really what you get from looking at me? A cookie-cutter, perfect life?"

"It's just a silly game I play in my head, smarty-pants. You try."

"I'm going to ignore the fact you just called me 'smarty-pants.' Right, let's see. I've just seen you walk past the window. You glance my way because, let's face it, I'm that good-looking." He cocked his head and wiggled his eyebrows, trying to keep a straight face.

"I was probably looking at Darren. He's better looking than you." I saw a flash of jealousy as he glanced over at Darren.

He continued. "You are by far the most beautiful woman I've

ever seen, but there's a sadness to you that I feel compelled to understand. Perhaps you've just broken up with your boyfriend or lost your job. I would run after you and ask you to have coffee with me."

"You have no idea how to play fair, do you?" I asked, shaking my head. "You were supposed to give me the perfect life, too."

"I did." He sat back on his chair and disarmed me with another smile. "You were about to meet me."

Smooth.

"What made you say I looked sad?" I couldn't help but ask.

"What made you say I was going to propose to my girlfriend?"

"Touché. So there wasn't any truth to it?"

Shut up right now, Holly. You're a freaking masochist!

"Your eyes. You have this face and body men would go to war over, but when you smile, it doesn't reach your eyes. Don't get me wrong, they're beautiful and sexy, but you can't hide the sadness behind them."

Who the hell says that to someone they just met?

My alarm bells were blaring. I had to escape. Was I really that transparent today? How was I going to hold it together during the presentation if a man I'd just met could strip me bare that easily?

"I'd better get going. It was nice to meet you, Ryan." I pushed back my chair and tried to stand up gracefully, but the strap of my laptop bag was tangled around my ankle. I nearly fell flat on my face. *Wow.* My exit from this man's presence was going to be as embarrassing as my entrance. I was horrified to feel my sad eyes welling with tears.

I just stared at him, and he stared back. The thought of never seeing him again actually made my chest ache. It felt wrong to walk away, but it seemed like the safest thing to do.

"Finish your coffee, Holly."

"I'm sorry," I replied, holding out my hand. "I really do have to go. It was very nice to meet you."

As he took my hand in his, I felt a bolt of electricity at the contact. Pulling away and stepping towards the exit, I couldn't resist a backward glance. His piercing blue eyes stared right at me. The physical attraction was hard to deny, but that's not why I had to leave. This man was dangerous territory for me.

Pausing to get some fresh air before going into work, I grabbed my phone from my bag and quickly typed a text to Audrey.

Got dragged into work today. Not good. Met ridiculously hot guy in the café. Will fill you in tonight x

Before I even made it to the entry foyer, Audrey had responded.

Oh Hol, hope you're okay. Work drinks tonight. Will see if you're up when I get home. Need details on café guy! Love you x

Chapter Three

"What took you so long?" Jason asked. "I told Slater you'd be right up."

I put my things down at my workstation. "I was just preparing myself. I'm here now."

"Well, Slater wants to see you right away."

"Holly, what are you doing here?" asked Eva, with her usual saccharine bite.

"Jason was good enough to inform me about the last-minute change with the Davenport meeting," I replied.

Eva "Bitch" McCormack. No prizes for guessing how she hoped to influence the decision to have her design chosen.

"You forgot to button your shirt up properly, Eva," I quipped.

Jason stifled a laugh behind her.

"Jealousy's a curse, Holly," Eva said, glaring. She placed one hand on her hip and prodded me in the upper arm with the other. "It doesn't suit you."

"Jealous? Why the hell would I be jealous of a crazy b–"

"Breathe, Holly," Jason's calm voice whispered in my ear as

he dragged me away. "She's not worth it. She's just trying to rile you up before the presentation. It's classic Eva – you know that. And you don't usually bite back."

Breathe in, breathe out.

"Well, I don't usually have to talk to anyone today, so she'd better watch her back."

"Feisty Holly is kinda hot," he smiled cheekily.

"Don't you start." I was momentarily transported back to my chance encounter with the uber-hot Ryan.

"Okay, not sure what you mean by that, but you need to get your butt into Slater's office right now."

Shrugging my shoulders in defeat, I took a few steps away from Jason. Stopping, I turned back. "What would I do without you?"

He gave me a warm smile. "Never going to find out."

I returned his smile, then made my way to Slater's office. Eva was already there, of course.

"Thanks for joining us, Holly," Mr Slater said, genuinely. "I know you booked today as annual leave – I hope you didn't have anything important planned."

Vitally important, but that was not information that needed to be shared with anyone, least of all my boss and my nemesis.

"It's absolutely fine. This is a big opportunity for me."

He nodded. "So, you both have your presentations ready. And remember, I'll be there to back you up." He stood up and gestured towards the door. "Let's head to the conference room for a run-through."

An hour later, I was well and truly ready for a breather from the suffocating presence of Eva and her breasts. Mr Slater, on the other hand, was mesmerised by them. It was fair to say Eva held the upper hand. The managing partner was showing clear favouritism towards the busty blonde, who would no doubt warm his bed if it helped her career. Hopefully Mr Davenport would choose my intelligent design and creative ideas for sustainability over Eva's cleavage.

"Okay, ladies, let's take a quick lunch break. Stretch your legs, and be back here in an hour."

The second Slater left the conference room, Eva turned on me.

"You don't stand a chance, Holly. I have this in the bag."

"What do they say about counting your chickens?" I retorted, wishing I could come up with something better.

Ignoring me, she pulled out her phone and started tapping away. "Have you checked out Mr Davenport online?" she asked, without looking up. "He is unbelievably hot. Makes our Jason look like a complete waste of time." Looking up from her phone, she flicked her hair over her shoulder. "When my design is chosen, I'm sure there'll be lots of opportunities for one-on-one time with him, discussing layouts. And by layouts, I don't mean –"

I cut her off. "Ugh… I know what you mean, Eva. I hate to break it to you, but you don't get to be the successful CEO of a multinational corporation by choosing inferior work based on who is going to warm your bed for one night. I tailored my design to complement the Davenport signature style whilst maintaining my own architectural stamp. If he prefers your approach, good luck to him." With my rant over, I collected my notes and stood up. "Oh and by the way, don't ever say 'our Jason' again." I quickly exited the room, leaving a shocked-looking Eva alone with her slutty thoughts.

When I got back to my workstation, I found Jason hard at work with his earbuds in, bopping his head to whatever music he was listening to. As if sensing my presence, he looked up, pulled out one earbud and gave me a heart-warming smile.

"Want to grab a bite?" I asked. "I don't have much time, but after what I just endured, it would be nice to have some decent company."

"Of course," he replied immediately. "Let's grab a sandwich and hit the gardens."

Our office was located one street away from the beautiful and tranquil Botanic Gardens. Jason and I often spent our lunch breaks running through the gardens and along the harbour foreshore. Sometimes we preferred to eat under one of the spectacular trees, surrounded by friendly white ibises. It was one of Mum's favourite places to take me. We would stare up at the buildings of the CBD, chatting about the architectural genius or lack thereof. Her passion had inspired me to be an architect, too.

"Er, not today." I tried to keep the rising emotion out of my voice. "Let's just grab a bite downstairs, okay?"

"It's okay to think about her, Holly." He put his arm around me, steering me towards the lift. "Come on. Lunch is my treat."

Chapter Four

As we walked into the café, I couldn't help glancing around the tables to see if Ryan was there. It was ridiculous, but I was having serious trouble keeping him out of my thoughts. I was embarrassed to acknowledge the explicit nature of these thoughts. *Seriously, get a grip, Holly.*

"Order anything you want. Go crazy," Jason joked. He knew full well I'd order the chicken salad like I always did.

"I'll have the ch– actually, you know what? I'll have the burger. Just call me crazy."

"Seriously?" Jason threw his arms in the air. "Thank God." He grabbed me by the shoulder and tried to keep a straight face. "It's pained me to watch you miss out on Darren's burgery goodness for this long."

I struggled to stop myself laughing. "I'm pretty sure 'burgery' isn't a word."

"It's totally a word. Wait 'til you try it. The only question you'll have is why you wasted so much time with beans and cat food."

Dropping his hands, Jason turned to Darren, who was grinning broadly.

"Hey, don't knock the niçoise," I interjected. "It's the best of the salads."

Inane as our chat might have been, it felt really good to switch off and enjoy some banter before the big presentation. Jason was my comfort zone, and I loved him for it.

Having inhaled his burger in record time, he wiped his mouth, then clapped his hands together. "Alright. It's nearly go time, superstar."

Mum used to call me superstar. Shit.

"I don't think I can do this, Jase." I rubbed my forehead, perhaps attempting to force out my negative thoughts. "I'm fine one second and then feel like I'm going to hyperventilate the next. I met a guy here this morning when I was getting coffee, and he said I looked sad. I nearly cried in front of him."

Jason grimaced slightly but didn't interrupt.

"I almost bit Eva's head off back in the office, and if anyone says anything that triggers a memory, I'll blow it. I know I will." A lump was forming in the back of my throat as I continued. "You know how hard this day is for me. It's just better if I'm away from people."

Jason pulled his chair across and put his arm around me. "You're going to be fine." He squeezed my shoulder reassuringly. "You're going to be more than fine. You go in there and show Mr Davenport why you are the greatest thing to hit the Australian architecture world since the legendary Anna Wilson."

I flinched at her name.

Jason must have felt my body tense. He pulled me around to face him and held both my arms. "You go in there and show Eva 'Bitch' McCormack why she will always be runner-up. But more importantly, you go in there and focus on the good memories of your mum."

I swallowed the lump in my throat, but my eyes still blurred as Jason continued.

"From what you've told me, she was strong and smart – just like you. Do this for yourself and for her. Tonight, we'll get really drunk."

"Thank you. I seem to be saying that to you a lot today."

"Just own this, Holly. Don't let today's date ruin it for you. Tonight, we'll celebrate."

We returned to the office in comfortable silence. I needed to get a hold of myself. Jason was right; I needed to own this. But first, I needed to freshen up, so I made a quick trip to the bathroom. Touching up my makeup in the mirror, I made a conscious effort to ignore the sadness my eyes refused to hide. My hair was being very well-behaved, so I made a quick decision to pull the elastic band out, allowing it to fall loose down my back. I could hear Audrey's voice in my head, reminding me to take advantage of my natural assets. I reapplied my pink lip gloss, pinched my cheeks for a bit of extra colour, stood up straight and pushed my shoulders back.

I was ready to face-off.

Chapter Five

Mr Slater appeared at the conference room door accompanied by the three Davenport representatives. One by one they filed into the room. As Slater began the introductions, I couldn't believe my eyes.

"Ryan Davenport, Michelle Cartwright and Piers Holloway, I'd like you to meet two members of the Slater Jenkins team. This is Eva McCormack and Holly Ashton."

What? No, no, no, no! This is not happening!

Ryan from the café as none other than CEO Mr Ryan Davenport, and he was standing right in front of me. I sucked in a loud breath as he shook my hand for a few seconds too long, piercing me with those eyes. I was stuttering when I managed to croak out my greetings. My eyes darted around the room, trying to work out if anyone had noticed my unprofessional demeanour. My brain was having a hard time catching up. When I dragged my eyes back to his, Ryan seemed calm and collected. He was a professional, and I was a silly girl, overreacting.

Once everyone else was seated, Mr Slater walked to the head of the table.

"Welcome," he began. "Firstly, thank you for choosing Slater Jenkins for this exciting project. I think you'll be really impressed with Holly and Eva's individual visions for your building."

Before Mr Slater could continue, Ryan interrupted him. "Ladies, before you present your designs, I'd like a brief idea of your background and a sense of your architectural style."

This was the last thing I needed. Talking about my past would take my brain places I needed to avoid today.

Own it, Holly. Breathe in, breathe out.

Eva stood immediately, clearly thrilled by the opportunity to talk about herself. I didn't mind. It gave me some extra time to compose myself.

"Thank you, Mr Davenport," Eva purred. She then proceeded to gloat about her exemplary academic record and various university accolades. She also felt it necessary to point out that she'd chosen architecture over a career in acting, like her father, the famous Marcus McCormack. Of course, the crazy bitch also managed to work that in. She was beyond reproach. During her speech and as she presented her design, I stole a few glances at Ryan. He was completely fixated on Eva. I had to admit she was impressive, and her talent was undeniable. Taking her seat, she looked directly at me and mouthed the words "in the bag".

She was going down.

"Okay, now we'll hear from Holly," Slater said, still smiling at Eva.

I stood up and pushed my shoulders back. Flicking my hair over my shoulder for good measure, I took a deep breath. Then, as if I had no choice, I made eye contact with Ryan. The way he was looking at me made my face flush. I felt the heat rise up my neck like an impending tsunami of panic. Perhaps sensing my distress, Ryan cleared his throat and asked me what the inspiration had been for my design. His calm, sexy voice settled my nerves, and I momentarily forgot my raging emotions. I also forgot about the other people in the room.

"My mother was my inspiration, actually."

"Really? Tell me about that." He seemed genuinely interested, giving me the confidence to continue.

"She's the reason I pursued architecture. She showed me how to look at things in ways I never would have done before."

"And what ways would they be?" Ryan asked.

"She taught me to look at things from every angle, not just the obvious ones."

Ryan's warm smile urged me to continue.

"Lie down on the footpath and look directly up at the building next to you. Do a handstand against a tree in the park and look back at the city skyline." The memories came freely. "Take a boat to the middle of the lake, then jump overboard. How does everything look when you first resurface?"

Ryan leant forward on the table, just as he'd done in the café earlier. My confidence grew.

"Whenever we were admiring a building," I continued, "Mum would ask me to tell her the thing I liked most about it. The first couple of times, I said the obvious things, like the colour of the bricks or the sandstone footings. But Mum wanted me to look for the less obvious things, the things I really *loved*. When I was studying your apartment building, I visited the site both during the day and at night. I watched the way the light refracted off the water and transformed its appearance. The water became the most important factor in my redesign concept."

I rambled on about my ideas and aspirations for sustainable living. It was all just a bit of a blur. Barely drawing breath, I eventually ran out of steam, and the room came back into focus. That's when I noticed the shocked look on Slater's face and the smug grin on Eva's.

I sat down, wondering what the hell I'd just said. It definitely wasn't what I'd rehearsed earlier.

As Slater discussed some of the more technical issues, I could feel tears welling in my eyes. Staring at Slater, I barely heard a word he said. I was just willing him to stop talking so I could get the hell out of there. I had never gone rogue by allowing my personal life to affect my work before. I refused to look at Ryan.

"I'm afraid that's all we've got time for," Ryan said. "I've got another meeting across town, but thank you so much for your time. I have your business cards." He handed Eva and me his card.

Our fingers touched briefly as I took the card. When I looked up, my eyes met his. I felt a heady combination of excitement, confusion and vulnerability. I had no idea what he was feeling, but neither of us smiled.

I was officially mortified. Had I really told them that I did handstands in the park? *Ugh.*

Slater saw them out and was in meetings for the rest of the day. I had no opportunity to apologise or attempt to explain. What could I say, anyway?

Chapter Six

After two quick glasses of wine and one slow one, my embarrassment was starting to feel more like a fuzzy memory. Slater had suggested we take the Davenport representatives out for drinks after work. Michelle and Piers accepted the invitation and agreed to meet us at the bar around six. Ryan said he would do his best to come despite his jetlag and back-to-back meetings.

"I'm sure it wasn't as bad as you think," Jason said, putting his arm around me.

"It really was," said Eva, laughing derisively. "Can you do a handstand for us now, Holly? You were very entertaining."

"Shut up, Eva," Jason warned. "You'd better pull your head in when the clients arrive."

"Don't worry about me, pretty boy. I plan to be Mr Davenport's sole focus. I won't be wasting my time talking about your buddy and her emotional baggage." Her sly smile made me want to smack her in the face. Fortunately, she sauntered off towards the bar before I could act on the impulse.

"Seriously, Holly," Jason said. "You need to cut yourself some slack." He picked up his beer and took a long swig. "I feel terrible for dragging you in today. Perhaps I should have let you have your day."

"You think?"

"God, Holly, I really thought I was doing the right thing."

Before I had a chance to respond, Slater, Michelle and Piers joined us. Apparently, Ryan was tied up in a meeting and would be joining us later. Eva cornered Piers, and I couldn't help smirking at her blatant flirtation. We spent the next couple of hours making small talk and drinking. I was having a pretty good time, thanks to the welcome buzz of the wine. The group grew larger as other colleagues joined us. When I glanced at my watch, it was almost ten o'clock, and the bar was packed and noisy. I was well beyond tipsy and really should have been heading home.

I pushed through the crowded bar, heading for the bathroom. As I passed a group of suited men, a hand grabbed my arm, jerking me to a stop. Annoyed, I looked up into a set of drunken, bloodshot eyes.

"Hey, let me go," I said, trying to pull away. Drunken suits didn't scare me, but his beer breath was disgusting, and I wasn't in the mood for this all-too-familiar routine. It was going to end with my knee in his balls.

"Do you know why they call this bar the Dry Cleaner?" he slurred.

"Err, no. Can you please let me go now?" I was increasingly concerned by his tight grip. He was hurting my arm.

"'Cause it's where you go to pick up a suit." His mates laughed at his dismal attempt at humour. He tried to pull me in closer.

"Let her go," a stern voice commanded from behind me. "She's with me."

He dropped my arm like it was on fire, and I turned, bumping into Ryan's imposing frame. Taking my hand, he guided me away from the drunken suit and into the hallway leading to the bathrooms.

"Are you okay?" His furrowed brow and darkened eyes looked concerned and angry.

"You are abnormally good-looking."

Holy shit, did I just say that out loud? Definitely too much wine…

Ryan grinned and took a step closer. "I like your hair down," he whispered into my ear. "Although it was a little distracting during your presentation."

While I was paralysed by his closeness, his comment shocked me back to reality. I thought about my mortifying speech in the boardroom and cringed.

"I need to use the bathroom, but you'll find everyone over there." Moving aside, I gestured towards the bar.

Leaning forward, he closed the small distance between us. "What's wrong, Holly?"

"You didn't have to save me from that guy. I can take care of myself. I take self-defence classes, you know. He would have gotten a knee in the balls if he hadn't let me go soon."

"I actually believe you," he said, laughing. "I had a feeling we'd meet again."

"Oh God, are you one of those hippy kismet types who believes in serendipity and the universe telling you things?"

"No. I just know what I want, that's all. It's what compelled me to approach you in the café."

"I thought it was the lack of other seating options?"

"You have a smart mouth, Ms Ashton."

I couldn't help looking at his perfect lips, which were now extremely close to mine. My breath hitched. My heart rate increased, and my breathing slowed with every second.

"I really want to kiss you."

I immediately knew I would let him. Was I out of my mind? If Slater found out I was fraternising with such an important client, he would fire me. No man was worth that risk. But there was something about *this* man. He made it difficult to think clearly. There was only room for one thought.

"I want you to kiss me." It felt like the truest sentence I'd ever spoken.

Ryan pressed his lips against mine, kissing me with an intensity I responded to immediately. I found myself pouring all the pent-up emotion of my day into kissing him back. A small groan sounded from the back of his throat as he pulled my hips closer to his, deepening the kiss. I looped my arms around his neck and ran my hands through his hair. This was by the far the best kiss I'd ever experienced. The electricity between us was almost unbearable.

When we eventually came up for air, I was immediately flooded with shock at what I'd done. What *we'd* done. I pushed him away and brought my fingers to my lips, trying to ignore the tingling sensation long enough to order my thoughts.

"Slater's not going to fire you."

Not only was he a phenomenal kisser, he was also a mind reader.

"I have to go. I'm sorry." I turned to walk away.

"This isn't over, Ms Ashton," he said with authority.

I turned. His expression was impossible to read. "Pretty sure it never began, Mr Davenport." Satisfied at having the last word, I turned on my heel and quickly made my way to the bathroom.

***

Once I'd freshened up, I made my way back through the noisy bar. I could see Jason and the others standing near the entrance to the courtyard. As soon as I touched Jason's arm, he turned and took a step away from the group.

"Oh my God, Holly," he said with concern in his voice. "I was about to come looking for you. You just missed Mr Davenport."

I took a long sip of the drink he handed me before responding in a casual voice. "Oh, really? He can't have stayed long." I desperately hoped it wasn't obvious how hot and flustered I was. "What did he have to say?"

Jason glanced over his shoulder. "No idea. He had a quick word with Slater, then left." He grinned cheekily as he sipped his beer. "Eva looked really pissed that he was oblivious to her existence. You would've loved it."

"Jase, I think I'm going to head home. Do you think I've put in enough time?"

"Absolutely," he said without hesitation. "I'll come with you." He sculled his beer and deposited the empty glass on the table next to him.

"Don't you want to stay and put the moves on the blonde by the bar?" I gestured towards the stunning woman who had been eyeing him since I returned from the bathroom. "She's gorgeous."

He just shrugged his shoulders and sighed. "I chatted to her while you were in the bathroom. She's nice enough, but I'm not interested." He held my coat out for me. "Let's go."

Just as I was buttoning up and getting ready to leave, Slater approached.

"Can I have a word, Holly?" He looked at Jason and raised his eyebrows. "A private word?"

Jason held up his hands, taking the hint. He made his way over to Michelle and Piers, leaving me alone with our boss.

"You just missed Ryan Davenport," Slater said when Jason was out of earshot.

"I know," I cringed. "Jason told me. Mr Slater, I didn't get a chance to say this after the meeting, but I wanted to apologise for my emotional outpouring during the presentation today. It's not like me to bring my personal life into work, and I'm sorry. I really hope I didn't embarrass you or the firm in any way."

Slater looked at me like I was from Mars.

"What are you talking about, Holly? You blew me away with your speech. I had no idea you had that in you. And you clearly blew Mr Davenport away, too. He chose your design."

My jaw dropped, rendering me speechless for a few seconds as my poor, sobering brain tried to process the enormity of what he had said.

"Um, really? I mean, seriously?"

Professional, really professional...

"Yes, Holly. Really. He'd like you to come to his office on Monday to go over your design in more detail. He was really impressed with you. Congratulations."

Still in a daze, I said my goodbyes, then Jason and I headed out. The whole city buzzed with people enjoying drinks after work. The later it got, the messier it got. It was only ten-thirty, but the streets were already full of drunken suits.

"I'll walk you home, then get a cab from Oxford Street," Jason offered.

"Sounds good to me. Thanks."

Jason wrapped his arm tightly around my shoulders, and we worked our way through the crowds.

"So what did Slater have to say?"

"That Ryan – I mean Mr Davenport – has chosen my design."

Jason stopped and turned. "Oh, that's amazing, Hol. Congratulations! Your design was perfect. Mr Davenport obviously has great taste." He hugged me tightly.

"Thanks, Jase. I'm still a little shocked."

When we reached my apartment building, I held my breath, hoping he wouldn't want to come up and hang out. I was exhausted. I just wanted to curl up in bed and recover from the day.

"Thanks for coming to get me this morning. Didn't turn out so bad in the end, I guess."

"You're welcome. For what it's worth, I think your mum would be proud of you regardless of your work successes."

I gave him a quick hug. "Night, Jase."

As I opened the front door into our quiet, dark apartment, I was struck by the view, as I always was. The wall opposite was floor-to-ceiling glass, and you could see right over Hyde Park to the city skyline, lit up in all its urban glory. I love beach and water views when I'm on holidays, but for me, there has always been something soothing about a cityscape. Maybe it's the architect in me.

Despite being emotionally drained, I lay awake staring at the ceiling. All I could think about was that kiss. I had never been so attracted to a man before, and I was finding it unsettling. I was no virgin – I enjoyed the company of men and I enjoyed sex. I just never allowed any kind of emotional connection. Serious relationships were of no interest to me. It was just safer that way. But with Ryan, there was an irresistible attraction beyond anything I'd experienced before. He made me feel completely exposed, yet strangely exhilarated, all in a single glance. It had me rattled. The fact that I was going to be working with him was terrifying.

Glancing over at the clock, I realised it was after midnight – I had made it through another birthday.

Chapter Seven

Instead of feeling relief at having survived the day, I felt… I didn't know how I felt. A light knock on my door jolted me out of my thoughts.

"Come in."

"Hey babe, just wanted to check that you're okay," Audrey whispered, crawling into bed with me.

"Honestly, Aud, I don't know. It's been a full-on day, and I'm all over the place."

"So is it hot guy related or work related?"

"Believe it or not, they're one and the same. Hot guy from the café turned out to be Ryan Davenport, CEO of Davenport Property."

"Holy crap, Hol. That's who your design was for, wasn't it?"

"Yes. What were the chances?"

"Sounds like fate to me."

I rolled my eyes. "Oh God, not you, too. Ryan thought the same thing."

She flicked on my bedside lamp, flooding the room with light.

"Holly Rose Ashton. Spill it."

Squinting, I pulled the bed covers over my face, trying to stifle a strangled laugh. When I edged them back and peeked over the top, Zara was there, too. So I was in for the Spanish Inquisition. *Excellent.*

"What's going on?" Zara asked.

"Nothing is going on. I met a hot guy today who turned out to be a client."

"Ryan Davenport. Let's google him!" Audrey suggested excitedly.

Zara tapped away at her phone, then showed Audrey the search results. I had to clamp my hands over my ears to drown out the squealing.

"Oh my God, Holly! He is a god," squealed Audrey. "You have to have sex with him, then tell us everything, so we can live vicariously through you."

"Yeah, like that's going to happen. I'm not going to have sex with him. He's a client. End of story. He's a really good kisser, though," I winked. I knew I was adding fuel to the fire, but I couldn't resist.

"Shut up!" they said in unison.

Audrey was suddenly serious. "Hang on a second. That's a bit risky, isn't it? Kissing a client is very out of character for you. Did it have anything to do with it being a particular day of the year?"

"That's what I was deliberating when you came in. I wasn't myself all day," I said. "We made some crazy, weird connection that totally freaked me out. Then, in my presentation, I found myself opening up to him about how Mum inspired my architectural style."

Audrey and Zara glanced at each other quickly but said nothing.

"Then he was at the bar tonight, and all I could think was how much I wanted him to kiss me." I touched my lips briefly. "Even though I knew it was wrong, I didn't care. The whole day was one big out-of-body experience."

Nervously pulling at the stitching on my bedspread, I glanced up. My two best friends were staring at me.

Audrey put her arm around my shoulders. "It sounds really romantic. I'm so happy someone is making a crack in the Great Wall of Holly."

Zara climbed off the bed and picked up a photo from my dresser of Jason and me at the go-kart track. "Jason will be jealous. Pretty sure he thinks he has the monopoly on you."

"Nothing is going to happen with Ryan. He chose my design, so I'm going to be working at his on Monday. It's not like I'm going to risk my career over a man."

"Oh my God! That's massive. Congratulations," Audrey said, hugging me excitedly.

"That's so awesome, Hol," Zara said, smiling. "You deserve it."

"Thanks, guys."

"I wonder how Jason will cope with you working with the smoking hot Ryan Davenport?" Zara asked.

"Jason and I are just friends. He says he's happy just hanging out with all of us."

"Well, you know him best, I guess. But I'm confident he's biding his time until you're ready to commit," Zara said.

"Don't worry about Jason. It'll be fine." I hoped that was

true. He, Audrey and Zara were my best friends, and I didn't want to hurt any of them, ever.

"It's so unfair," Audrey complained. "Why can't my work colleagues look more like Jason – or Ryan, for that matter? I'm surrounded by the kind of specimens you find at the singles table at a wedding."

"Wait, so let's get this straight," Zara said. "For the first time in a long time, you let down your defensive wall just a little and put yourself out there on the one day of the year you normally hole up with ice cream and TV. On this particular day, you also happen to have a massive win at work, and you kiss a sex god. That's got to tell you something, right?"

"It's time, Holly," Audrey added.

I had a nauseating feeling of déjà vu. "Time for what, exactly?"

"It's time to break your own rules and let someone in. You're missing out on life," she continued.

"Don't argue, Hol. Just think about it, okay?" Zara said.

They both hugged me and then left before I could respond.

Knowing sleep would elude me for a while yet, I reached for my bedside drawer and took out a box. It had been a long time since I last ran my hands over the smooth, dark wood. My fingers traced the initials engraved into the lid: ARW. Anna Rose Wilson. We shared a middle name, as well as many physical features. Lifting the lid, tears immediately welled in my eyes. She looked back at me from the photo I had stuck to the underside of the lid. She was a beautiful woman, tall and slim with light-brown hair that hung in glossy waves down her back. I got my darker hair from my father, but my distinctive eyes came from Mum.

These physical features, however, were not what made her so breathtaking. She was lit from within. That's what I remember about her. Everyone she met loved her, and her energy was infectious. Wiping away the tears, I picked up her charm bracelet. It was the one piece of her jewellery I had asked to keep. Each charm reminded me of a time with her that I treasured. We found our favourite one at the London Silver Vaults on Chancery Lane when I was ten years old. Carefully, I held the silver oyster and opened it up to reveal the tiny pearl inside. I remembered her delight as she first discovered that it could be opened. I hadn't thought about her infectious laugh in so long.

Still holding the bracelet, I picked up my journal. Lifting it to my nose, I breathed in the nostalgic smell of leather and was immediately flooded with memories of Mum teaching me to ride a horse. The smell of the tack room, full of saddles and bridles, was intoxicating. Slowly peeling back the soft leather cover, I read the poem I'd written for Mum's funeral service almost a decade ago.

You're safe on your pedestal, Mum. You're frozen in time.

A beautiful life snuffed out in its prime.

My heroine, my teacher. You were my protector and friend.

Life going forward, I just can't comprehend.

You were creative and generous. You were thoughtful and kind.

I can't help feeling you've left me behind.

What will we do now, from our own private hell?

These words are nothing more than a reluctant farewell.

Breathe in and breathe out, one step in front of the other.

My broken heart's bleeding for the loss of my mother.

I ran my finger over the words and was stabbed with the familiar mixture of emotions – grief, anger and betrayal. This poem had become my armour, deeply etched into my damaged heart.

Chapter Eight

Snatched from sleep by a buzzing sound, my brain eventually worked out that my phone was vibrating on my bedside table. The lamp was still on, and my journal lay open on my chest. I was still clutching Mum's charm bracelet; it had made tiny impressions on my palm. My head was pounding and my eyes were puffy. Trying not to move too quickly, I reached gingerly for my buzzing phone. "Hi, Dad."

"Hi, sweetheart. I just wanted to say happy birthday for yesterday. I know you don't like us calling on the day…"

"It's okay, Dad. How are you?" I asked, feeling the tightness in my head worsen.

Each year, the grief Dad felt on the anniversary of Mum's death was exacerbated by the guilt he felt for not wanting to celebrate my birthday. We spoke irregularly and said very little. Every time we spoke, I was reminded of how much he missed my mother and how lost he was without her, just like I was. It wasn't what he said – it was what he didn't say. He was distant and detached, a shell of his former self. In the years following her death, I tried to hold it all together for my sisters as much as I could. But for Dad, I knew I was a constant reminder of her. It felt like every time he looked at me, he slipped further into his grief. When I finished school, I moved out and went to university. I saw them less and less. It seemed better that way.

"I was hoping you could come over tomorrow for lunch. April and Jamie will be there, and Connor, of course. We haven't had a meal together in ages. Bring Audrey if she'd like to come. I'd love to see her, too."

"Um, yeah, okay, sure. Sounds good. I gotta go though, Dad."

Collapsing back on my pillow, I sent Jason a quick text asking if he wanted to go for a run. I had given up trying to make Audrey and Zara run with me years ago. They preferred exercising at the gym. Something to do with the muscly personal trainers, no doubt. But Jason and I both loved to run. Today, I was hoping it would help clear my foggy head. His reply came quickly – he would meet me in twenty minutes.

I scribbled a note for the still-sleeping Audrey and Zara, then made my way downstairs and across the road into Hyde Park. My thoughts turned to Ryan. I couldn't help wondering what he would be doing this weekend. *Where does he live? Does he have a girlfriend? Why am I wondering if he has a girlfriend? Do I want to be his girlfriend? Why am I wondering these things about a client? What's wrong with me?*

Completely lost in my thoughts, Jason surprised me with his usual, affectionate greeting. The man liked to hug.

"Hey, gorgeous. How's your head?"

"Hoping a run will sort me out."

"Right then, let's go. Try to keep up," he said, sprinting off.

We always took the same route on weekends – past St Mary's Cathedral and the art gallery, then around the harbour foreshore to the Opera House. *Spectacular.*

Jason was fit. Really fit. Keeping up with him was a bit of a struggle, but I enjoyed the challenge. The best strategy was to send my mind elsewhere, away from the burning in my muscles. Unsurprisingly, I thought about Ryan. There was no doubt I was attracted to him. Of course I was. He was ridiculously handsome. But there was something more that drew me in. When he looked at me with those deep, blue eyes, I felt beautiful and desired, but I also felt… weak and out of control. I stopped suddenly at the realisation.

Bending over, I put my hands on my knees, desperately drawing air into my lungs. I was going to be working for a man I was wildly attracted to and had an unprecedented connection with. That was bad enough. But something about Ryan Davenport made me think it would almost be worth throwing my career away just to have one night with him.

What the hell?

"You okay?" Jason put his hand on my back.

I just nodded, then straightened up and started jogging again, a little slower this time. We were almost back to Hyde Park anyway. I knew I wouldn't make it if I spoke even one word. As soon as we got back to our starting point, I collapsed in a heap on the grass. Sweat was pouring off me, and I felt a little dizzy. Jason, on the other hand, looked like he could run the same route all over again. He lifted his white t-shirt and wiped a thin layer of sweat from his brow, revealing his tanned six pack. Staring at Jason's abs, I found myself wondering what it would be like to run my hands over Ryan's chest and abs. Jason smirked at me, then held out his hand to help me up.

As we wandered back towards my apartment, I felt him looking at me.

"What?" I asked meeting his eyes.

"There's something different about you today. I can't put my finger on it."

"Different how?" I asked, genuinely curious.

"Well, for a start, you've never looked at me the way you did when I lifted my shirt. Looked like you were checking me out." It was obvious from his grin that he was happy about it.

The flush rising from my neck was unavoidable. He'd caught me staring. Explaining it was the problem. I needed to find a way to shut this conversation down before I did any real damage.

"Err… it was just that Audrey mentioned something about you the other day, and I was just thinking about that. Don't read anything into it, pretty boy."

"So what did Audrey say about me?"

"Oh, she was just complaining that none of the men asking her out were as hot as you. Don't go getting a big head now. You're not that hot." I punched him gently on the arm to reinforce our friendship-only status.

"So Audrey thinks I'm hot?"

"Surely you knew that? She hasn't exactly made a secret of it."

Jason didn't say anything. When I glanced over at him, he seemed a million miles away.

"Hey, Jase. Can I ask you something?"

Shaking his head as if he was trying to empty out the

thoughts, he looked at me, smiling warmly. "Of course."

"Why don't you ask Audrey out?" He appeared completely blindsided by the question.

"Are you serious? We're friends. It's not like that. Geez, Holly, where is this coming from?"

"You started it by asking if I was checking you out."

"Well, I regret it now. Can we drop this? Are we getting coffee?"

"Come upstairs and we'll grab Aud and Zara."

Chapter Nine

The four of us spent the rest of the day together. On Saturday night, we went to our favourite club, Moon, where Zara's quasi-boyfriend, Jake, was the DJ. I couldn't help noticing Jason looking quizzically at Audrey. Perhaps I had planted a seed there? Audrey was a great dancer, and guys couldn't help being mesmerised. Jason seemed to be noticing her in a different light for the first time. I quickly shut down a brief flash of jealousy. I knew it was hypocritical to expect him to remain single if I couldn't offer him the kind of relationship he wanted. He and Audrey would make an amazing couple.

Audrey, Zara and I had taken a ridiculously long time getting ready to go out. Jason had sat in our lounge room, groaning every time one of us changed our minds about our outfit.

I had finally settled on my black jeans and silver sequined, off-the-shoulder top.

"You look perfect, Holly. Can we please go?" he begged.

Audrey had incredibly long legs and made the most of them, wearing a killer black dress – short with a low-cut back. Zara was the most risqué of the three of us. At first glance, the nude slip dress made her appear naked. In a million years, I wouldn't have had the confidence to wear that, but she owned it.

Jason looked particularly handsome in his dark jeans. The black t-shirt he wore wasn't tight, but it gripped his biceps, hinting at the toned body underneath. If I was willing to have a serious relationship, perhaps I would have risked our friendship to see if something could happen between us.

"Can I buy you a drink?" I was interrupted from staring at Jason and Audrey by the standard pick-up line.

"No, thanks," I replied, then turned to see a surprisingly attractive guy.

"Just one drink and a five-minute conversation. After that, you can go back to watching your friends have a good time. What do you say?" I couldn't help smiling. And who said I couldn't have a little fun? Meeting Ryan had fired up something in me that I'd never experienced before. Given that I was going to be working for him on Monday, I needed a good distraction.

"One drink then," I conceded. "Vodka cranberry."

"I'm Sam, by the way."

"Holly. It's nice to meet you, Sam." As I held out my hand, he boldly brought it to his lips. I looked him in the eye. There was no doubt Sam was a good-looking guy. His dark hair was cut short. His eyes might have been brown or maybe a really deep green. Being in a dark club made it difficult to tell. But there was an unmistakable flash of lust in them. I was attracted to him, though there was none of the electricity I'd felt with Ryan.

Stop it, Holly. Forget about Ryan! Focus on the hot, available, uncomplicated guy right in front of you!

As soon as Sam headed off to the bar, Zara accosted me.

"Um, who was that fine specimen?" she asked.

"Sam."

"What happened to the forbidden fruit of Mr Sex God, Ryan Davenport?"

"Seriously, Zara. You just said it. Ryan is forbidden fruit – I can't think about him. Sam is going to help me with that."

Sam reappeared with my drink. "One vodka cranberry, as requested."

I quickly introduced him to Zara, and he politely shook her hand.

Zara turned to me and winked. "Don't do anything I wouldn't do. Have fun, kids."

With that, she skipped off towards Jake in the DJ box. I could see Audrey, by now commanding quite a crowd of admirers on the dance floor. Jason was still watching her.

"So, Holly. What is it you do?" The music wasn't deafening, but we still had to talk almost directly into each other's ears to be heard.

"I'm an architect for Slater Jenkins."

"Oh wow, that's impressive. I hear that's a difficult firm to get into."

"Don't tell me you're an architect, too?"

"No. I'm a structural engineer at Tresswells."

"Oh, right. What do you specialise in?"

"Residential mainly, but I've been involved in a few commercial projects recently." He took a sip of his beer. "Do you really want to talk about work?"

"Err… I guess not. Sorry. I can get a little one-track when it comes to work."

"Don't apologise, Holly. I love talking shop, but it's getting a bit too noisy in here. Can my five-minute conversation be extended to one dance?"

I was so interested in his work that I had forgotten my five-minute deal. Despite the lack of chemistry, I was having a good time with Sam.

"Sure, why not?" I replied, letting him take my hand and lead me onto the dance floor.

When we were completely surrounded by jostling bodies, Sam pulled me into him. He started to move with a rhythm that not many guys possess. I was no Audrey but I could hold my own, and I enjoyed escaping into the music that was pumping through my chest. Wrapping my arms around his waist, I could feel the muscles in his back flex. I found myself enjoying the power I seemed to have over him and decided to push a little further. We were already dancing extremely close, but I closed the tiny gap and could feel the tightness at the front of his jeans.

Sam's lips were on my neck, and his hands made their way to my backside, gently pulling me further into his body. It was already hot in the club, but we were both starting to sweat from the heat rising between us. Sam leaned down and looked directly at me, our lips not even an inch apart.

"You are so hot, Holly." Our lips connected and I closed my eyes, hoping to feel even a fraction of a lightning bolt. Sam was a good kisser, and I was determined to lose myself in him completely. I gently pulled back from the kiss and rested my head on his chest.

"Can my one dance be extended to a drink somewhere quieter?" Sam whispered in my ear.

This was the point of no return. I wanted to stay lost in him, so I nodded my head against his chest.

Knowing a quiet drink could lead to his apartment, I didn't allow myself time to overthink it. It was just casual, emotionally-detached sex – my comfort zone.

Sam held my hand and waved to a group of guys as he led me towards the exit. I caught Zara's attention. She shrugged her shoulders but nodded her head in understanding.

***

We stopped at a nearby bar. It was clear neither of us were particularly interested in a quiet drink or much conversation. Instead, we opted for a couple of shots. They helped eradicate any awkwardness a quieter location with a virtual stranger may have brought, along with any thoughts of my new client. Sam was great fun. He told so many jokes that my sides ached from laughing until I cried. I was buzzed.

"Can a drink somewhere quieter be extended to a tour of my apartment?" he asked, moving his hand slightly further up my thigh. "I live just around the corner."

I was ready for some steamy action from this smoking-hot guy. "Lead the way."

Sam's eyes darkened as he stood up, grabbed my hand and led me towards the door. In typical form, I stumbled on a ridge in the carpet and fell forward. Fortunately, Sam managed to prevent my fall, and we left the bar laughing at my clumsiness. I'm sure he was hoping I was less clumsy in the bedroom.

***

Sam's apartment was a quintessential bachelor pad in a modern apartment building overlooking Cockle Bay. I'd drunk enough to have a good time but not so much that I failed to appreciate the building. By coincidence, Slater Jenkins architects had designed it, and Tresswells construction had completed the build, about a year ago. I had never seen inside any of the apartments and was impressed by the interior design and high-end fit out. The furnishings were minimalist and monochromatic. He could have done with a woman's touch to add a sense of warmth. However, I was from the "less is more" school of design, so it was generally appealing to my critical eye. I couldn't help wonder what Ryan's apartment would look like. *Shit.*

Sensing my distraction, Sam pushed me against the lounge room wall and kissed me hard on the mouth. His hands made their way to my backside. Once again, I could feel his erection straining in his pants, and it pressed into me. With the wall against my back and Sam's hips grinding into me, I tried to shut my mind down and lose myself in the moment. His tongue greedily explored my mouth. My sequinned top was wrenched over my head, causing a few slightly awkward moments. I would no doubt be finding rogue sequins in my hair the following day. Breaking away briefly, he quickly rid himself of his own t-shirt, then resumed his exploration.

The guy knew what he was doing. It just wasn't doing it for me. My mind was working overtime on providing interference. The way I'd felt when Ryan kissed me in the bar was all-consuming and highly confusing. I knew I had to get him out of my mind, but this wasn't the way to do it.

Sam's hands moved to my zipper. I stopped him gently.

"I'm sorry, Sam." I looked into his eyes so he could see that my apology was genuine. "I can't do this now."

"Really?" He took a step back and put his hands on his head.

"I… um… I'm not feeling great." It wasn't a lie. I did feel mildly nauseous. "I think those shots are disagreeing with me."

"Oh man, I'm going to need a cold shower now." He smirked so I knew he wasn't pissed off with me. "Are you sure?" He stepped forward and attempted to kiss me again.

Placing my hands on his bare chest, I pushed against him gently. "I'm really so sorry. Can I use your bathroom, please?"

Once I'd composed myself in his bathroom, I found Sam in the kitchen. He was leaning back against the counter sipping coffee.

"Coffee?" he asked, giving me a warm smile.

"No, thanks. I might head home," I replied, returning his smile. "I'm just going to call myself a cab." I pulled out my phone and started scrolling through my contacts.

"Can I get your number, Holly? I had a really good time with you tonight, even if you are a tease." He chuckled to himself.

He was a nice guy. This could have gone badly – not all guys would have taken my change of heart as well. I gave him my number, and he immediately dialled it so I would have his number, too. Sam was a fun, casual, good-looking guy. He was safe. Once I had sorted my head out, I'd be happy to see him again.

Chapter Ten

"Did you have a good night?" I asked Audrey when we eventually surfaced for a caffeine hit mid-morning.

"Yes and no," she replied, taking the coffee mug I offered her. "The music was great, and there were a few cute guys. One in particular – a surfer from the northern beaches."

"That's great. So what was the problem?"

"It's probably nothing." She appeared awkward and unsure. "Jason was a bit weird at the club. I caught him looking at me strangely a few times."

"Oh," I said sheepishly, staring into my coffee. "I may have told Jason you think he's hot." I clenched my teeth and scrunched up my face.

Her whole demeanour relaxed, and she took a swig of her coffee. She laughed a little. "I tell him that all the time. Why would that be news to him?"

"That's what I thought. But when I told him yesterday, he seemed surprised."

"That's strange. He friend-zoned me ages ago."

"That's just it, though. I think he may have been re-evaluating that last night."

"Wouldn't you find that awkward? You two are like an old, married couple."

"Just make sure you break up amicably is all I ask."

"Why do you always assume things are going to end, Holly?"

"Because they always do. I just don't want to lose either of you in the fallout."

"Enough about me. Talk to me about the guy you left the club with."

"Sam." I took a big gulp of my coffee. "Sam was… fun." I glanced up to see her shaking her head. She seemed disappointed in me.

"So Ryan is off the menu then?" she asked, shaking her head. "I was kind of hoping you'd see where that could go."

"Well, I didn't end up sleeping with Sam. I just couldn't get Ryan out of my head."

Audrey smiled as she spread Vegemite on toast.

"There's no chance I'm risking my career over a guy, though, no matter how hot he is. Anyway, Sam is fun. I gave him my number." As I took a bite of my toast, savouring the salty goodness, I suddenly remembered my conversation with Dad. "Oh, I almost forgot. Any chance you want to come to lunch with my family today?" I asked, feeling a bit guilty that it had slipped my mind.

"Oh, sure, I'd actually love to come. I haven't seen your dad and sisters since April's twenty-first. When was that?"

"Um… April."

"Oh right, sorry. I'm a little bit hungover here," she replied with her eyes shut, hitting her forehead with her hand.

"Righto. Well, we're due there around midday. I'll drive." I put my coffee mug in the dishwasher and wiped the crumbs from the bench.

"What time is it now?"

"Ten thirty. Plenty of time to become presentable – well, for me anyway. I clearly didn't drink as much as you."

"Ugh. Thanks a lot."

Smiling, I handed her another cup of freshly-brewed coffee. She breathed in the fumes as if they alone could cure her pounding head.

***

Dad still lived in the same house my sisters and I grew up in. Everything about it had Mum's stamp on it. It was impossible to escape the vivid memories in every room. I found the place both eerie and comforting, although I flat out refused to go into the master bedroom. Jamie was in high school and still lived at home. Technically, April still lived there, too, but according to Jamie, she didn't spend many nights at home. She had been with her boyfriend Connor for four years now, which seemed insane to me. They were so young.

Despite finding my family home a place of mixed emotions, I loved the street. Large liquidambars lined the street, forming an avenue of leaves. I had fond memories of April and me collecting cicadas in a box and climbing those trees with our friends – completely carefree. I don't remember a single adult in any of those memories.

"Is that a For Sale sign outside your house?" Audrey asked as I was parking.

"No way. Dad would've told me." A feeling of dread suddenly

swept over me as I walked towards the house. Audrey was right. A large sign had been erected, emblazoned with a picture of the back verandah overlooking the swimming pool.

"I'm guessing that's what today's conversation topic will be." Audrey put her arm around my shoulders. "You okay?"

"Of course. I thought he would have done this years ago." Why was I lying to my best friend, who would have completely understood my horror?

Dad met us at the front door with warm hugs.

"Hi, Mr Ashton," Audrey said.

"How many times have I told you to call me George?" Dad replied. His warm smile conveyed the genuine love he felt for her.

"Sorry, George. Old habit, I guess," Audrey replied.

"What's with the sign, Dad?" I asked, trying to appear unaffected.

"Come inside, Holly. April, Jamie and Connor are out the back. We'll talk over lunch."

Dad was a great cook and had made his signature lasagne for lunch. Once we were all seated, he tapped his wine glass to get our attention.

"Okay, guys. As you all now know, I've decided to sell the house. In fact, I accepted an offer yesterday, so we'll be moving out in six weeks. Letting it go was obviously a difficult decision, but it's the right time. I've come to realise it's just bricks and mortar. Our memories are in here." He left his hand over his heart while he continued. "While I remain here, I'm stuck in the past, and it's time for me to move on with my life. You girls have made me so proud. It's time for me to start living, too."

"Have you bought another house?" I asked, forcing my voice to sound upbeat and casual, masking my inner turmoil.

"I've bought a two-bedroom apartment at Balmoral Beach," he replied. "I know how much you girls love it there."

"It's really gorgeous, Hol," April said. "You'll want to visit all the time."

"That's great, Dad." I was trying so hard to be happy for him.

He smiled warmly at me, then raised his wine glass. "To letting go and moving on."

"To moving on," everyone repeated. I opened my mouth, but the words stuck in my throat.

When everyone started to eat, I excused myself to use the bathroom. I just needed a few minutes to compose myself.

As I returned to the table, Jamie called out. "Hey, Hol. Remember that time you chained yourself to the tree in the backyard when it had to be cut down?"

Smiling at the memory, I replied, "Of course I do. Would have worked, too, if Mum hadn't lured me inside with chocolate cake."

"What about the secret passageway?" April asked. "How did we not get bitten by funnel-web spiders crawling through there?"

"I always worried about that," Dad said. "It was your mother who insisted we leave you alone to be adventurous explorers."

It went on like that throughout the rest of lunch. We had so many memories in that house, and most of them involved Mum.

How could he sell Mum's house?

Chapter Eleven

I woke up on Monday feeling tired, yet determined. By the time I had showered, dressed in my go-to black suit, done my makeup and inhaled my coffee, I was almost ready to face my first day at Davenport Property. I had a plan. My defensive walls were firmly back in place, and I was on track to be the best damn architect they'd ever employed.

Ryan and I had connected on a level I hadn't thought possible, but that had been on a day when I was weak and vulnerable. Today, I was back in control. The weekend away from him had given me the perspective I needed to push him back to where he belonged – at arm's length.

Just as I was about to head out the door, my phone buzzed. I had programmed Ryan's number from his business card, so I immediately knew who the message was from.

Can I give you a ride to work?

Surprised, but shamefully thrilled, I replied: *If it's on your way? I'm in the Hyde Park Apartments on Liverpool St.*

His response came through almost immediately. *I'll be there in 5.*

I was frustratingly excited to see him. *This was not part of the plan.* After double-checking my makeup and giving myself a little pep talk in the mirror, I called goodbye to the girls and headed out the door. Leaning back against his dangerously sexy, charcoal-grey Aston Martin, Ryan set my body on fire. His smile let me know he was as happy to see me as I was him. *Definitely not part of the plan.*

Stopping just beyond arm's length – at least that was part of the plan – I drank in his incredible good looks. As I took in his light grey suit, worn over a crisp, black shirt, my thoughts were inappropriately sinful. They involved a ripped black shirt. Clearly, I needed a new plan.

"Well, you got even more beautiful over the weekend." His sexy voice jolted me out of my fantasy.

"That's strange. You look just the same," I replied, trying to regain my composure. "I could have caught the train, you know."

"I'm sure you could have, but I think you'll find my car more comfortable than the vinyl express at peak hour."

"Well, thank you, I guess…"

Davenport Property's offices were located across the Harbour Bridge in North Sydney. I loved crossing the bridge and knew that I would have lived on the north side if it weren't for Zara's apartment in the city. I felt more at home in the north. Even though it's full of memories, it's where I grew up.

We pulled into the underground car park, and Ryan expertly manoeuvred into one of the reserved spots. Neither of us made a move to get out. Once we were in the office, we would need to be in full professional mode.

The sexual tension was palpable. I wanted him to kiss me again. When he looked at me, I knew he wanted to kiss me, too. We stared at each other, each daring the other to make the first move.

I broke first, looking down at my hands, which I was nervously wringing in my lap. "This cannot happen. I'm working for you." Out of the corner of my eye, I could see he hadn't broken his intense stare. "You are my client," I continued, meeting his gaze. "This just can't happen."

"Who are you trying to convince, Holly?"

"You. I mean, me. I mean… well, both of us, I guess." My mind was a jumble. I needed some space from him. As if sensing my need, he was out of the car and opening my door before I could finish a complete thought.

"Come on." He reached for my hand, and I took it instinctively. "Let's go upstairs."

We rode up to the office, smirking at each other in the mirrored elevator walls. I had absolutely no idea how I was going to pretend there weren't fireworks going off between us.

As the doors opened, he placed his hand on my lower back and gently nudged me forward. His touch was so intimate that my whole body shuddered.

"Don't touch me, please," I whispered, not looking at him. He removed his hand.

"Good morning, Mr Davenport," said the perky, young receptionist. I held back a chuckle. Her flirting was not of the subtle variety. But really, who could blame her?

"Good morning, Chloe." His response was unaffected and professional. "This is Holly Ashton. Can you please show her around and make sure she has a workstation set up?"

"Of course, Mr Davenport," replied Little Miss Perky. "Is there anything else I can do for you?"

"No, that's all. Just make sure Holly has everything she needs. Thank you, Chloe." Striding off, I couldn't help staring at his sexy swagger. I found myself wondering what sort of desk he had and what we could do *on* that desk.

Get a grip, Holly, you have a plan. Okay, a flailing plan, but a plan nonetheless.

"You can put your things here." Chloe motioned towards an empty workstation by the window. After pointing out the amenities, she introduced me to the other employees. Michelle Cartwright and Piers Holloway had their own offices and greeted me warmly.

The day passed in a blur of meetings. Everyone seemed genuinely enthusiastic about my design, although a few of my ideas would need to be reined in, courtesy of some feedback from the finance department. Oblivious to the darkened sky outside, I was completely engrossed in reworking one of my drawings when I felt his presence behind me. I glanced at my watch and was surprised to see it was after six o'clock.

"You're so sexy when you're concentrating."

I swivelled around in my chair and lost myself briefly in his lust-filled, sapphire eyes. *My God, he's gorgeous.*

"Are you all done for the day?" I asked.

"I'm done with work, that's for sure. Have dinner with me?"

Even though I knew we were alone, I still glanced around the empty office, a little flustered.

"Like a work dinner?"

"Of course, Ms Ashton," he replied with a grin.

"Alright then. Dinner."

Nice plan, Holly.

Shaking my head but unable to keep the corners of my mouth from turning up, I quickly saved my work and shut down my laptop. Allowing him to carry my things, we returned to his car and headed south.

"You were amazing today, you know," Ryan said, after a few minutes of silence.

"Thank you. I really enjoyed being at your office."

"I've cleared it with Slater so you can work out of my office for the rest of this week."

I just stared out the window, catching glimpses of the Opera House as we crossed the bridge. My mind flashed back to the time Mum took me on a behind-the-scenes tour of the iconic building. We'd gotten up at the crack of dawn for the seven a.m. tour, and it had been worth the early start. Mum and I were both mesmerised by Jørn Utzon's inspired design. He had been a young architect when he won the competition with his design for the Sydney Opera House. I wasn't arrogant enough to compare myself to him but I did aspire to greatness, and I was determined to leave my mark somehow. Ryan's intoxicating presence was making me consider jeopardising my career. I needed to sort that out quickly.

He glanced over at me. "Where did you just go? I lost you for a minute there."

"Oh sorry, um, that's fine. Working at your office this week. Got it."

We had dinner at an Italian restaurant in Darlinghurst.

Despite making no further attempts to touch me, he was making my plan to stay professional and emotionally detached very difficult to carry out. I was incredibly drawn to him and not just because he was so physically attractive. He had a sharp wit, a creative mind and was a complete gentleman, which I was mostly happy about, although part of me wanted to rip off his clothes and ditch my stupid plan altogether. What was happening to me?

"So tell me, Holly," he said, as our coffees arrived after our plates had been cleared away. "How is it that a smart, funny and gorgeous girl like you is single?"

"I could ask you the same question. How is it that *you* are single?"

"Firstly, I asked first. And secondly, who says I am?"

The look on my face must have given me away.

"I'm kidding, Holly. I'm single. I'm not in a hurry to be tied down. So…?"

"So… that was a great meal. Have you ever been to Italy?"

"Nice try. No deflecting."

Sighing, I sank down in my seat slightly. "I'm not interested in serious relationships either. I'm focused on my career." It was an honest answer, and I hoped we could leave it at that.

"If I tell you something, do you promise not to laugh?"

"No. I will definitely laugh. That's like saying 'promise you won't think about pink elephants'. It's impossible not to do something when you're told not to. That's a well-known scientific fact."

"Okay then. I won't tell you."

"No, you have to now. Another well-known fact is that you can't ask a question like that and then not spill it."

He leaned back in his chair and crossed his arms over his chest. "Wow, Holly. What must it be like to be your brain?"

"Spill it, Davenport." I gave him my sternest look, making him laugh.

"Okay, okay." He uncrossed his arms and put his elbows on the table. "I spent the weekend formulating a plan to keep my professional distance from you today."

"Really?" I shocked myself with my composed response. "And how successful was your plan?" Butterflies were rioting in my stomach. It seemed we really were on the same page.

"Well, that depends on your perspective," he replied, flooring me with his dazzling gaze.

"It was your plan. Surely there's only one perspective?"

"No, what I mean is from a professional perspective, it went really well – I haven't yet crossed any lines. But I desperately want to take you home and rip your clothes off, so it's also going really badly."

"Oh." Staring at each other across the table, my mind went into a death spiral. What was I supposed to say to that? The heat in my cheeks burned, and I could no longer risk looking him in the eye. He would be able to see my shaking resolve.

"It's not worth the risk," I whispered. But when I glanced up and met his eyes, I immediately questioned that statement.

Ryan signalled to a passing waiter for the bill.

"Look, Holly." He reached across the table and took hold of my hands. "I don't play games. I like you. You are a beautiful, sexy, talented woman, and I'm not going to deny being out-of-my-mind attracted to you."

I blushed at his compliment and pulled my hands back, placing them on my heated cheeks.

"What are you trying to say?" I whispered.

"I'm not sure exactly. I guess I don't agree about it being such a great risk. We seem to both want the same thing here – neither of us is interested in anything serious."

"Just sex, no relationship to complicate it. Is that what you mean?" I asked, trying to keep my voice as even and unaffected as possible.

"Let's get out of here." He stood and held out his hand. I took it, which felt a lot like agreeing to his suggestion.

Ryan settled the bill, ignoring my attempts to split it with him. I didn't push the point – it was, theoretically, a work dinner.

There were cabs lined up outside the restaurant, but neither of us made a move towards them.

"Thanks for dinner." I had no idea what to say or do.

Ryan stood directly in front of me and tilted my chin up, leaving me no choice but to look him in the eye.

"Tell me what's going on in that crazy brain of yours, Holly."

"So much. Too much. Possibly not enough? I'm confused, I guess."

His lips touched mine, and incredible sensations took over my entire body. I was insanely affected by this man, but I just wasn't sure an emotionally-detached fling was possible.

"We both know it will be amazing. Give it some thought. But don't take too long." He kissed me again, then led me to the cab at the front of the queue.

As my cab pulled away, I stole a glance out the back window. Ryan was standing where I had left him with his hands in his trouser pockets. He caught my eye and smiled. I smiled back. He knew. I knew. There was something special between us.

When I got home, Zara and Jake were cuddled up on one couch watching TV. Audrey and Jason were on the other couch, a platonic distance between them.

"Long day?" Jason asked. "How was it at the Davenport offices?"

"It was actually really fantastic. I've had to make a few changes to my design, but it's exciting. Mr Davenport has asked me to work there all week. How did Eva take the loss?"

"Not well. A toddler throwing a tantrum would be one way to describe it. But Slater asked her to help him with one of his other projects, so that shut her up."

"Ugh. Glad I didn't have to witness that."

"Have you eaten?"

"Um, yes. Ryan, I mean, Mr Davenport, took me out for dinner."

"Oh really?" Zara chimed in. "Well, wasn't that nice of him." She turned to Jake. "Holly is working for the sexiest man alive, Ryan Davenport."

"I thought *I* was the sexiest man alive," Jake said, kissing her neck.

"Of course you are, babe," Zara said, winking at me.

After a shower, I flopped down on my bed and stared out the window at the city lights, blurred by the misting rain. It was only ten o'clock, but it felt much later. Trying to process what was happening to me was near impossible. Closing my eyes, I felt myself drifting off to sleep with a smile.

Chapter Twelve

Getting ready for day two at Davenport, I felt lighter somehow. Perhaps it was the fact that I had enjoyed working there so much the day before. Perhaps it was because I felt like my career was taking off, or perhaps it was the excitement brewing about my chemistry with Ryan. Whatever the reason, I decided to wear a skirt. Audrey was always telling me I should wear skirts to show off my legs, but I usually opted for the more conservative trouser suit option. As I smoothed my pencil skirt down, an image flashed through my mind. It involved Ryan and the skirt pooled at my feet. Holy cow, my mind was firmly in the gutter.

I wandered across Hyde Park and through the city to Town Hall station. I hated the train, especially at peak hour. We were jammed in like cattle, with no choice but to invade each other's personal space. As I made my way to the Davenport offices, I found myself surprisingly nervous about seeing Ryan, yet desperate to see him at the same time.

As I put my laptop down at my workstation, I glanced around the office and could see at least half the employees were yet to arrive. I looked over to Ryan's corner office. The door was closed, so I couldn't tell if he was in yet. Part of me had been disappointed when I realised he wasn't waiting outside my building this morning, but I had quickly pushed those thoughts out of my head.

Today, my only strategy was to get on with my work and try not to let my mind wander. No more daydreaming about Ryan hovering over me naked with hooded eyes.

Seriously, Holly. That is not helping!

For the next few hours, that's exactly what I did. I barely looked up from my computer and was surprisingly productive. All my experience with detaching my emotions meant it was easier than I'd expected.

"Hi." He startled me, and I shivered at the sound of his voice.

"Hi," I replied, swivelling my chair around. I was still taken aback by his raw beauty. It may sound strange to describe a man as beautiful, but that's exactly what he was. His commanding frame emanated a rugged strength that was complemented by his clear, dark eyes, which were currently undressing me with their gaze. They must have been – I suddenly felt like ripping my clothes off.

Seriously, snap out of it, Holly!

"Sorry I didn't pick you up this morning. I had an early morning conference call with the London office. Hope the train was bearable."

"Totally bearable, thanks. I'm perfectly capable of getting here myself."

"I'm not trying to threaten the feminist movement here, Holly. I enjoy your company. Is that a crime?" He was grinning, so I knew he wasn't irritated. He also glanced down to my skirt, which had ridden a little higher when I crossed my legs.

There goes my contribution to the feminist movement. Using my body to flirt with a man.

"Can I see you in my office?" he asked, appearing mildly pained.

Pushing my skirt down and my shoulders back, I followed him, walking as casually as I could. When I reached his office, he was leaning back against his large, black desk, his legs crossed at the ankles.

"What can I do for you?" I asked coyly.

"You can close the door for a start." I closed the door, then paused for a few seconds with my hand resting on the handle, trying to muster some mental strength before turning around.

"So, I'm all yours."

"Interesting choice of words, Holly."

"I meant… we're in private now. What did you want to talk to me about?" I took a couple of steps towards him, and his eyes raked down my body. I should have felt objectified, but instead I felt empowered by the appreciative look in his eyes.

"You should wear skirts more often. You have great legs."

"Thank you." I wore it for you.

"I've booked a table for us to have lunch on Friday at a venue just north of Sydney."

"Oh, okay. Sounds lovely."

"It's a stunning property, and it's won countless environmental awards for its luxury accommodation. It reminds me of your design concept for my apartment building."

"Oh… Right… Okay…" My whole body flushed at the mention of accommodation. I felt dehydrated suddenly.

"Excellent. I know the owner, so I'll arrange for a full tour."

The magnetic draw to him was stronger than ever, and my body was screaming at me to be pressed up against him. As if he could read my mind, he stepped forward and ran his hand across my cheek. The hairs on the back of my neck stood on end, and my whole body tingled at his light touch. My desire for him was overwhelming.

"Come on, we're going on an Aqua Vue site visit. I know you've been there, but I'd like to take you there myself. I love the location even more since hearing your presentation."

Davenport Property had bought an old apartment building on the harbour foreshore next to McMahons Point ferry wharf. Extensive building works had already been undertaken to ensure it was structurally sound. The guts had essentially been ripped out, and the building was ready for a whole new layout. My design was for eight luxury apartments, each taking up one of the graduating levels. The design took advantage of the incredible water views whilst also minimising the environmental impact.

As Ryan drove us the short distance to the site, he fired questions at me about my ideas on design and the current architectural trends – my favourite topic.

One of the reasons I loved the Aqua Vue site so much was the view of the CBD skyline from the north. The hundred-and-eighty-degree view captured Luna Park fairground directly across Lavender Bay, then the Harbour Bridge, across to the CBD and then down towards Darling Harbour. From here, you could feel you were a part of the city while still being removed enough for a tranquil perspective. A cold breeze rushed up off the water, and Ryan immediately put his arm around me.

"I love this view," Ryan said, quietly.

"Me too. I was just thinking that."

Ryan smiled at me, then stared out across the water.

"I'm going to keep one of the apartments when the building is complete," he said, still not looking at me. "So this development is personal."

"As a kid, I loved Luna Park." Ryan raised his eyebrows, obviously surprised. "I loved the scary rides. The roller coaster was terrifying, but the adrenaline rush was like nothing else. I was a bit of an adrenaline junkie as a kid."

"Did something happen to change that?" His arm seemed to tighten around my shoulder.

"I grew up, I guess. I like to be in control of my own actions. I don't enjoy things being beyond my control the way I used to. Does that make sense?"

"I like being in control, too. I love running my own company. But sometimes you have to let your hair down and have some fun, too. What do you do for fun, Holly?"

"I hang out with my friends. I run. I go out for coffee. I walk through old buildings."

"Can you add casual sex with your boss to that list?" He was laughing.

I elbowed him in the side. "You're not my boss; you're my client. And there's no way I would ever have sex with Slater."

We both laughed, and I realised how much I enjoyed hearing his laugh. I shook my head. I enjoyed everything about him. His physical presence was overriding all my senses.

"So, I'm meeting my friends for a few drinks after work." I had no idea why I was telling him that. The words just tumbled out of my mouth. "We'll probably get dinner together. You're welcome to join us, though I'm sure you have better things to do."

"I'd like to meet your friends."

"Right, of course, okay then, excellent." I rubbed my forehead, knowing I sounded like an idiot. How was I going to keep this casual if I let him penetrate my personal life? Then again, we hadn't started anything yet, so it would just be dinner with friends.

Looking across at Luna Park, I could feel the adrenaline coursing through my veins. Mum had loved the roller coaster, too. We must have been on it a hundred times. The rattly cars of the Wild Mouse would propel us forward to certain death before jerking around the corner at the last second, only to hurtle down a steep decline. Mum and I would scream and laugh – usually at the same time. I laughed aloud at the memory, and Ryan looked at me curiously.

"What's so funny?"

"Nothing. I just remembered something."

"You're a confusing woman, Holly Ashton."

I couldn't help laughing, despite my instincts screaming that spending more time with him was a bad idea. However, the fighter in me was temporarily knocked out. My heart was winning.

The afternoon went by quickly, and I left the office around five with the rest of the staff. Ryan asked me to text him the details of where to meet. It felt an awful lot like a date, even though my friends would be there. What the hell was I doing?

Chapter Thirteen

I couldn't help smiling on the train ride home as I thought about Ryan. Watching him in action at work was like foreplay. He commanded the room, had the respect of all his employees and was exceptional at his job. It was a major turn on. Perhaps that was it. I was attracted to Ryan Davenport the powerful CEO, not Ryan Davenport the man. But that didn't make sense. When I met him at the café I'd had no idea who he was, but I was drawn to him, both physically and mentally. One thing I knew for sure was that this man was leading me down a dangerous path, yet I couldn't seem to make myself turn around. If anything, I felt the urge to start running faster.

Audrey, Zara and I caught a cab to Surry Hills. I had told them Ryan would be joining us, issuing strict instructions not to make a big deal out of it. It was not a date. We were friends.

We sat at the bar while we waited for Ryan to arrive and ordered three glasses of white wine.

"So what's going on here? Are you still trying to sell the 'there's nothing going on with Ryan' line to us?" Zara asked as she sipped her wine.

"We're just trying to work it out," I replied, a little defensively.

"I've never seen you so tied up over a guy before. You're usually so... I don't know... cold and detached?" Audrey said.

"Ouch." I knew she was right, but it still hurt a little to hear it. I was trying to protect the guys I dated by not letting them get too close. But Ryan was different. I knew it. They knew it. I stared into my wine glass. "Okay, well, I admit I'm attracted to him, but how could I not be? He's gorgeous, incredibly sexy and on top of that, you should have seen him in the staff meeting today. I had to go to the bathroom to freshen up afterwards – he made me so hot and flustered." I looked up to see Audrey and Zara looking behind me and smiling nervously. "He's right behind me, isn't he?"

They both nodded, unable to control their chuckling.

My face flushed immediately. I couldn't bring myself to turn around.

"So I make you hot and flustered. Good to know," Ryan said, sitting down on the bar stool next to me. "Hi, I'm Ryan. You must be Audrey and Zara." He leant across me and shook their hands. "It's nice to meet you."

"You too. Holly has told us a lot about you." Zara winked and Audrey laughed.

I really need to find some new friends!

Ryan received immediate attention from the bartender, who I was certain had been checking him out. While he ordered a beer, Audrey, Zara and I had one of our epic three-way silent conversations using eye movements, lip shuffles and eyebrow raises. In less than thirty seconds, they confirmed his hotness. I confirmed my desperation for them not to embarrass me and that I was happy he was there. Then they confirmed their happiness at my happiness. We needn't have bothered – Ryan's phone started ringing. and he excused himself to take the call.

"You're smitten, Holly Rose," Zara said as soon as Ryan was safely out of earshot.

Feeling an immediate flush in my cheeks, I gave her a half-smile. It was true. For the first time in my life, I felt my fragile heart was in serious danger. It was terrifying.

"And that, my friend, is a man in love," Audrey said, pointing to the door.

"Don't be ridiculous. Please don't even say that. I'm already freaked out enough, and I really don't want to overthink it."

"Good. The only thing you should be overthinking is how many different ways you can have sex with him."

"Zara, shoosh!" I begged. "He's coming back."

His blue eyes kept finding mine as he returned to his seat and continued to win over my friends. I liked watching him engage so effortlessly with them. I tried desperately to concentrate on the conversation, but my mind was one-track and dirty. I was overcome by a confusion I'd never before experienced with a man. I gave my forehead a gentle rub trying to ease the tension I was feeling.

Everything was blurring, and I had no idea what to do about it. Crossing the professional line seemed like the least dangerous part of my predicament. It was the way I felt in his presence that rocked me to the core. And yet, I desperately wanted to find a hotel and discover how it felt to get naked with someone who affected me so wildly, even when fully clothed.

"What's wrong, Holly?" Ryan whispered in my ear. "You look stressed."

"I'm fine."

"You're worrying about the superhuman strength it's going to take to keep our hands off each during dinner, aren't you?" *Is he a freaking mind reader?*

Fortunately, before I was forced to answer him, Audrey suggested we head to the Thai restaurant next door. I jumped down from my bar stool and grabbed my bag.

Jason had texted to say he wasn't going to make it – he was swamped at work and didn't know when he could escape. I was quietly relieved.

Temporarily suppressing my confusing feelings for Ryan, I managed to have a really good time throughout the meal. The bill arrived while Audrey and Zara were using the restroom. Ryan picked it up as if he intended to take care of it, but I snatched it from his hands. "I don't think so. Not two nights in a row. I'll get this one."

"Okay, my feisty friend," he said sardonically. "This is definitely *not* a work dinner."

"No. This is um… friends… having a friendly dinner with friends?" *Smooth, Holly. When did you get so eloquent?*

Ryan laughed. "You're so beautiful." He seemed shocked to have said it out loud.

"Um… thanks?" I stuttered in response. I knew he hadn't meant to say it, but I liked hearing it. *Really* liked it.

When Audrey and Zara returned to the table, Ryan and I were staring at each other in silence. But this wasn't an epic silent conversation. I had no idea what was going through his mind, and I really hoped he couldn't actually read mine.

"Well, it was lovely to meet you ladies," Ryan said to Audrey and Zara when we were outside on the sidewalk.

"You too, Ryan. You picked a winner here with our Holly. She's an incredible architect and the most amazing person I know," Audrey said with a quiet sincerity. "I may be a little biased though."

"Couldn't agree more," Ryan replied. He gave them both a kiss on the cheek, then turned to me. "Thank you for dinner."

His smile lit up his entire face and completely disarmed me. I desperately wanted to kiss him. He took a step closer to me and ran his right hand gently down my left arm.

"You're welcome. I had a good time with you." I blushed and had to look away from him. Holly and Zara had already flagged down a cab and were climbing in, so I took a step backwards towards them. "I'll see you tomorrow, Ryan."

"I'll pick you up at eight."

"I'm happy to get the train. I told you, I don't need…"

"Settle down. I'm not trying to deprive you of the joys of public transport. I'm going past your apartment anyway, so it's no bother."

"Okay. Sorry, I guess I'm used to being independent."

He took a step towards me and spoke against my cheek. His breath felt like kisses on my skin. "Have you given any thought to our conversation last night at dinner?"

I stared at my feet. "A little." *I've thought of nothing else.*

He tilted my chin up so I was forced to look him in the eye. "And?"

"And… I'm attracted to you. I'll admit that. But I'm just not sure about maintaining a professional working relationship at the same time. Do you really think it's possible?"

"I absolutely do." He kissed me properly on the lips, and my legs turned to jelly. "Friday lunch. We'll have absolute privacy, and if lunch turns into dinner, we can stay overnight if we choose. No pressure."

I just nodded, unable to form words.

"I'll see you in the morning." He kissed me again. The sparks already raging through my body were set alight. I thought I might spontaneously combust.

"Okay," I croaked as he pulled back and smiled. I stumbled ungracefully backwards, bumping into the door of the cab. Cringing, I composed myself, then opened the door and tried to climb in with poise. *Seriously...*

As the cab pulled away, I glanced out the window and gave Ryan a small wave. He held his hand up and smiled. I *really* liked him.

Chapter Fourteen

I had lived my life with a dogged determination to succeed as an architect, following in my mother's footsteps. I had also made a conscious decision to take the road opposite her when it came to love. Her career led to beautiful buildings and timeless structures. Her death led to a crumbling mess of despair. I could control my career, and I could minimise the collateral damage if I suffered the same fate as my mother and those before her.

My dad lived with a grief he would never overcome. The only thing that had ever made any real sense to me was to stay emotionally detached from men and focus on my career instead. It had worked perfectly – until now. Until Ryan. This man, who on paper was a complete disaster for me, was making me feel things I'd never felt before. It was truly frightening because it threatened both paths. Yet I found the lack of control strangely exhilarating.

I reached for my journal, suddenly compelled to write in it for the first time in almost a decade.

The words flowed easily, and I was struck by how cathartic it was. Emotionally drained, I must have fallen asleep mid-sentence. When I woke, I was shocked to see it was two in the morning. My journal was on the floor, and my pen was making an inky mess on my bedspread. *Great.* I ignored the mess and went back to sleep.

Chapter Fifteen

The next two days at work passed quickly. I didn't see a lot of Ryan, but whenever he was in the office, I was fiercely aware of his presence. He drove me to and from work both days. When he dropped me home on Thursday night, he said he'd pick me up at nine the next morning. Other than a kiss on the cheek, he hadn't made another move to kiss me again. I knew he was giving me time to make a clear decision.

Sam, the guy from the club, texted me a few times and asked if we could catch up again on Saturday night. I told him I was too busy. It wasn't a lie – I was desperately trying to work out what the hell I was doing with Ryan Davenport.

True to his word, Ryan was waiting for me at nine sharp the next morning. When I walked out of my apartment building, I was stopped in my tracks by the sight of him leaning back against his sleek Aston Martin Vantage – my new favourite car. As he stalked towards me, my whole body came alive with exhilaration and anticipation.

"Hi," he said in a soothing voice, despite looking like a predator about to go in for the kill. Suddenly, I felt like a zebra facing off with a lion. I needed to snap out of it. *Be the lioness, not the freaking zebra, Holly… you are not his prey!*

"Hi," I squeaked. *Freaking zebra…*

Ryan was a seriously good driver. I enjoyed watching him as he expertly navigated the Sydney traffic. I imagined his brain assessing the combined horsepower of the cars ahead to decide which lane to take - I found that sexy. Soon we were pulling up out front of a luxury apartment building in Rose Bay.

"This is my parents' place. I just need to pop up and see Dad quickly before we go. Do you mind?"

Are you kidding me? I'm not meeting your dad!

"No, not at all," I replied.

The door to the apartment was open when we got there, and a male voice called out to us from the kitchen. I felt incredibly awkward, but I decided to pretend I was someone else and just go with it.

A man who was unmistakably Ryan's dad appeared in the lounge room. He had the same intimidating stature as Ryan, and their eyes were almost identical. The silver hair gave him a distinguished look. There was no doubt he was a handsome man, especially for his age, which I guessed was around sixty.

"Hello, son." He shook Ryan's hand but was looking at me. "Who is this stunning beauty?"

"Dad, this is Holly Ashton. She's my architect for the Aqua Vue project. Holly, meet my dad, Daniel Davenport."

"It's very nice to meet you, Holly." He unashamedly looked me up and down, making me very uncomfortable.

"It's nice to meet you, too, Mr Davenport," I lied and took a step back. I could have sworn I smelled alcohol on his breath.

"Please, call me Daniel."

"Holly, do you mind waiting here a minute? I just need to talk to Dad about a few things in private, and then we'll be off." I could tell Ryan was uncomfortable with his dad's flirtation. I was relieved he was taking him to another room.

"Make yourself at home." Daniel winked at me as he left the room. *Ugh.*

I wandered around the expansive lounge area picking up various knick-knacks. There were a lot of knick-knacks – to the point of clutter. Every surface had something on it, but there was no real theme or thought given to colour or proportion. Daniel certainly didn't strike me as the knick-knack type, so I had to assume it was Mrs Davenport's doing. *To each their own*, I thought to myself as I noticed a row of framed photos on the bookshelf.

I loved looking at other people's photos, especially people I don't know; the shameless voyeur in me was always drawn to them. There were various photos of kids at the beach, happy snaps at the top of the Empire State Building, graduation ceremonies and so forth. Ryan obviously had a sister, as she featured in all the family photos. I was starting to think I'd had him pegged when I played my 'imagine-their-life' game in the café. He should've been more impressed with my mad skills.

"Ready to go?" Ryan asked, jolting me from my reverie.

"Yes." I looked at Daniel sheepishly. "Sorry, I hope you don't think I was snooping looking at your photos. I couldn't help myself."

"Not at all. You're welcome to come back anytime, with or without my son." He winked at me.

Ugh.

Ryan cleared his throat and took my hand protectively.

"Don't forget to go to that meeting, okay? Call me if you need anything," Ryan said to his father, patting him on the back.

"Have fun, kids," Daniel said, closing the door behind us.

"Sorry about that, Holly," Ryan said as we exited the building. "Let's go. We'll leave the car here and walk down to the marina."

At the bottom of Daniel's street, we crossed the busy road and made our way across the grass to the serene waters of Rose Bay. I was surprised by how natural it felt to be holding hands with this man. Despite the inevitable nerves, I felt overwhelmingly happy in his presence.

"Are we going by boat?" I asked, immediately thinking it was a stupid question, given the marina in front of us.

"Of sorts," he replied cryptically. "I hope you're not afraid of heights?"

"No, but I'm pretty sure heights aren't an issue at sea level."

I was rewarded with his sexy grin.

"This way," he said, guiding me further along the jetty, where hundreds of beautiful yachts and power boats were moored.

I was about to quiz him further when I noticed the seaplane moored to the end of the dock. I suddenly understood what he meant.

"Oh my God," I exclaimed, giddy with excitement. "Is this how you treat all your employees?"

"Not a chance." His laugh was contagious.

"Good morning, Mr Davenport, Ms Ashton."

"Morning, Gary," Ryan replied, shaking hands with the pilot, who then helped me aboard. We were both set up with headphones. Taking off on Rose Bay and soaring up over Sydney Harbour, I felt like I was having an out-of-body experience.

Ryan seemed to delight in my constant gasps as I pointed out a million different things. He knew from my presentation that I loved seeing things from new angles. I couldn't help wondering if that was a factor in his choice of lunch destination. My heart warmed at the thought. The diagonally-placed ceramic tiles covering the Opera House glistened in the sunlight, and I revelled in the beauty of my city.

Nowhere in the world compared to Sydney. I was fiercely defensive of it and of Australia in general. Passing over the heads, we flew towards the northern beaches, then headed up the Hawkesbury River. I had no idea where our destination was. At that moment, I simply didn't care. I was having the time of my life, and I wanted to enjoy every second of it.

Gary expertly landed the seaplane on the slightly choppy waters of the Hawkesbury, then slowly powered over to a private jetty where we disembarked. Despite only being a twenty-minute flight from the city, the surroundings couldn't have been more different to those we left. The humble-looking restaurant was nestled into a hilly backdrop, and a row of palm trees lined the shore. With no roads or alternate access points, the only way here was clearly by boat or air. It was truly serene.

Chapter Sixteen

We were greeted by a beautiful girl who looked to be around my age. Shoulder-length, blonde hair framed her fine features and pale green eyes. She looked like one of those athletic models from the surf wear ads.

"Hey, Gem," Ryan greeted her with a familiar hug. "This is my friend, Holly."

He turned to me. "Holly, this is Gemma. Her parents own the Hummingbird. She went to school with my sister, Aspen."

As we walked along the jetty, Ryan and Gemma chatted casually. They obviously knew each other well. Gemma ushered us towards the outdoor tables, where a waiter immediately welcomed us with cocktails.

"Let me know if you need anything, Ryan," Gemma said, smiling warmly. "Nice to meet you, Holly." She disappeared.

He handed me a cocktail, then held his up to make a toast.

"To chance encounters."

"Chance encounters," I repeated, looking him dead in the eye as we chinked glasses.

He broke my gaze and stared out towards the water, taking a

long sip of his drink. He appeared to be giving something a great deal of thought.

"I've got to head back to London soon for an important investor meeting."

The prospect of him being out of the country stirred an emotion in me I wasn't yet willing to confront.

"Do you spend much time in London?" I asked, trying to sound as casual as possible.

"Five years ago, I moved over there to open a London office. A few months turned into a few years. I now alternate between Sydney and London. It just depends on where the business needs me most. I love London, but Sydney is my home."

"That's great. I mean… I love London, too. I've only ever been once, on a holiday with my family. A lot of my friends spent a gap year there between school and university, but I was so focused on being an architect, I didn't want to waste any time. In hindsight, I wish I'd travelled more."

"There's nothing wrong with being focused on what you want, Holly." Ryan was now looking at me intently. "You just have to find a balance. You might find things you didn't even know you wanted."

Glancing out at the tranquil view, I tried to reconcile my turbulent emotions.

"Let's go inside and get some lunch." He took hold of my hand and squeezed it gently.

As we walked past a giant chessboard, the irony wasn't lost on me. Until I met Ryan, my life had been safe and predictable. I was completely in control of my emotions – mainly because I kept them safely locked away. Now I felt like a pawn, vulnerable to being taken out by a more powerful force.

Lunch was an incredible seven courses of gastronomic delights, intensified by matching wines. We chatted effortlessly about architecture and construction.

"Can I ask you something personal, Holly?" Ryan asked, looking me directly in the eye.

"Um, well, that depends on what it is," I answered coyly.

"Right," he said, smirking. "Well, I'll ask anyway. Is there a reason you're not interested in serious relationships?"

His loaded question wiped the smile off my smug face.

"Why are you asking me that?"

"Classic deflection technique. Try again." He folded his arms across his broad chest and leant back in his seat, smiling.

"I've already told you. My career is really important to me. I want to focus on doing the best job possible for you. The lines are already blurred… It's just too risky." That was honest. It just wasn't the whole truth.

"I've only known you a week, but I think there's more to it. Don't get me wrong, I feel like I've hit the jackpot here. I'm just interested in your reasons."

"Do you want to tell me *your* reasons?" I asked, raising my eyebrows.

"Not really." He paused for a few seconds. "I'm more accustomed to women who want more than I'm willing to give. And yet, with you…"

"With me… What?"

"With you… Well, let's just say I've never been so attracted to a woman before. I think about fucking you all the time."

My mind went blank. Well, that's not entirely true. My mind went directly to graphic images of Ryan's gloriously naked body pressed up against mine, doing unspeakable things to my willing body. *No shock there.*

Before my brain got a chance to override my dirty thoughts, the waiter suggested we take our coffee at one of the outside tables. *Perfect timing!*

The late afternoon sun was starting its descent over the eucalypt-covered hill behind the restaurant. It was getting colder, and the light was fading fast. We sat down at one of the outdoor table settings as our coffees arrived.

"Thank you so much for lunch." I sipped my cappuccino gratefully, trying not to be awkward.

"You're very welcome, Ms Ashton." He chuckled as he sipped on his own coffee.

"What's so funny?"

"I just told you I want to fuck you and you're in professional mode."

"Jesus Christ, Ryan. I have no idea what I'm doing here. Can you cut me some slack?"

He stood up and reached for my hand. "Come on. It's time for a tour."

When I stood up, he pulled me close. Our faces were inches apart. My breath hitched and my face flushed. My traitorous body leaned in towards him. Overruling it, I took a step back and headed for the path leading to the private beach. As I walked away, I took some composing, deep breaths.

Ryan caught up to me and grabbed my hand. I let him hold it as we walked the rest of the way to the sand. *Why does it feel so natural to be holding hands?*

As we turned the corner at the end of the path, five stunning riverfront apartments came into view. My architect's brain immediately kicked in.

"Wow." The apartments were gorgeous, blending seamlessly into the tree-covered hill behind them.

Ryan pulled a key from his pocket when we got to the last one. "This is ours for the night, if you feel comfortable staying. No pressure."

After unlocking the door, he stood back so I could enter, pressing his hand lightly on my lower back. I hated how much I loved the intimate gesture. Part of me just wanted to find the bedroom and ravage him immediately.

The unit epitomised understated luxury with a homely charm. The scent of fresh flowers mingled with the salty air from the river was an intoxicating blend. It made me feel a little light-headed. The architect in me appreciated the clean lines and sympathetic use of materials, which seemed to welcome the outside surrounds. The latest in sustainable technology had been employed wherever possible. I had already noted the rainwater tanks and solar panels on the other units. The layout made the most of cross-ventilation and the year-round sun. It was exactly the type of design I had described in my presentation, and I was thrilled to see such a beautiful example of sustainability in this incredible location.

"I love it, Ryan." I couldn't contain my grin. "Shall we check out the upstairs?" I willed my face not to turn crimson at my forwardness.

"After you." As I had suspected, upstairs we found the king-size bedroom with adjoining ensuite. The bedroom had glass sliding doors leading onto a balcony with uninterrupted views of the river.

"This is almost exactly how I had envisaged the Aqua Vue apartments." I felt elated.

Ryan nodded, smiling. "I know."

The evening mist rolled in across the river, making for a spectacular, yet eerie, sight. Standing on the balcony, leaning against the railing, I was completely mesmerised by the water. Ryan slipped away and returned with two glasses of red wine.

"Are you trying to get me drunk, Mr Davenport?" I asked in what I hoped was my sexy voice.

"Not at all, Ms Ashton." He gently grazed the back of his hand across my slightly-flushed cheeks. "You are so very beautiful."

"Thank you," I whispered, forgetting about the water. The view I had right in front of me was so much better.

I couldn't stop staring at his perfectly-shaped lips as they caressed the wine glass.

Without a word, he took my glass and put it on the table, along with his own. Placing his hands on either side of my face, he looked me directly in the eyes, our lips inches apart. "I've wanted you every second of every day since we met."

I was a goner. Ryan Davenport was consuming my thoughts, and I wanted to lose myself completely in his body and his mind. Suppressing the distant alarm bells, I closed the gap between us. When our lips collided, the anticipated fireworks erupted – Catherine wheels and rockets exploded behind my eyes in bursts of colour and light. Small groans escaped from both of us. Ryan's arms quickly enveloped me, pulling my hips into him. His erection was clearly evident as my body pressed greedily against his. It was the most erotic kiss I'd ever experienced, and I was damned if it was going to end there. I had crossed the line – I wasn't stopping now. He had cleverly let me make the first move, but when I started to pull at his shirt, he grabbed my hands, immediately halting my one-track mind.

"Are you having second thoughts?" I asked, irritated that he had ruined my bliss.

Ryan's arms immediately pulled me closer. He kissed my neck, then whispered in my ear, "I want you more than I want to breathe."

I pulled out of his arms so I could look at him. "I can't overthink this, okay? This is just sex. Nothing more, nothing less."

"Calm down, Holly. This is happening." He laughed, but his eyes were blazing. "I was just going to suggest you call Audrey to let her know you won't be home tonight. I got the impression she's quite protective."

I raised an eyebrow, conceding the point. "Audrey will love you for this."

"I'll be back shortly. I've got a few calls to make, too." He kissed me lightly, then retreated through the balcony door.

I watched him disappear down the stairs before grabbing my phone from my pocket.

"Hello," she yelled into my ear. I was momentarily deafened by the thumping music in the background.

"Where the hell are you?" I shouted.

"Hey, Hol, hang on, I'll go somewhere quieter."

I waited on the line as the music faded.

"Okay, that's better. So, tell me you're staying overnight with Mr Sex God."

"We're trying the casual thing. I might be making a massive mistake, but it's just sex, right?"

"Don't overthink it, Hol. You want him, and he obviously wants you. Just do it."

"So where are you now then? Somewhere noisy, from the sounds of it."

"Jake's having a party. He and Zara are currently doing what they do best. Jason's here with me. He seems a bit pissed off that you're spending all this time with Ryan."

"Oh, for God's sake, it's nothing serious. Tell him to get over himself. I've got to go, Aud. I'll see you tomorrow, okay?"

Resting my forearms on the railing, I stared out at the boats quietly rocking on the calm water. Each one was illuminated by a single light, providing a silent warning from the bow. This really was the most gorgeous place I'd ever been. Completely private, cut off from everything and everyone.

I was suddenly aware of Ryan's presence. I turned to find him standing at the balcony door.

"Come inside, Holly."

Like a magnet drawn by his irresistible force, I moved slowly towards him. Without another word, he took my hand and led me into the bedroom. My heart began to race. He scooped me up into his arms and brought his lips to mine as he gently lowered me onto the bed. The sexiest man I'd ever known hovered over me with hooded eyes. I'd already fantasised about this exact moment. The reality was so much better.

"I overheard what you said to Audrey." His eyes flashed with lust. "You're wrong about there being nothing serious going on here. You are seriously hot. And I am seriously going to fuck you until I hear you scream my name."

His words were like an aphrodisiac. My body was a trembling mass of sensation, and we were both still fully clothed. He gently swiped my hair away from my neck, exposing my skin to a trail of soft kisses. I wrapped my arms possessively around him, instinctively arching my neck to give him better access.

He tugged my shirt up and over my head before his mouth quickly resumed its exploration of my neck and shoulders.

His hand traced my collar bone and ventured down between my breasts. My need for him was becoming increasingly urgent with every passing moment. When his mouth met mine, I sighed in relief, despite the sensual overload. Our soft, gentle kiss quickly became greedy and lust-filled. His hand snaked behind my back and deftly snapped open my bra, lowering the straps over my arms, then discarding it.

Breaking the kiss, he propped himself up on his elbows on either side of me, his eyes roaming freely over my naked chest. "You are spectacular, Holly."

His mouth closed over my left breast while his thumb teased my right. I gasped loudly as an electric current jolted through my whole body. I wrapped my arms around his neck, pulling him closer. I'd never been so turned on in my life. My hips jerked upwards until I could feel his whole body pressed against mine. I was left with little doubt about his desire for me as it pushed against my thigh.

Pushing my hands up and under his shirt, I ran my fingers down his firm chest, pausing at his stomach. His defined abs flexed under my touch. He sat up and discarded his shirt in a blur.

I was beyond caring about what this meant. We were two consenting adults, wildly attracted to each other.

"Do you want me to fuck you, Holly?" he growled. He dropped his head, and I felt his next words hummed against the skin of my throat. "I need to be inside you. I've thought about this for too long to hold out much longer."

Before I could reply, he kissed me hard. He demanded entrance and I opened my mouth, letting his tongue slide over mine. Without breaking contact, my breathing became increasingly erratic as his thumbs hooked into the waistband of my trousers and pushed them down my legs. I managed to kick them off so he could return his attention to my mouth. His suit trousers and boxer shorts disappeared in a move that confirmed his experience in the bedroom. Pushing away concerns about not living up to his expectations, I grazed my fingernails down his smooth, muscular back, luxuriating in his sublime body. This man was a god.

"Say it, Holly. I want to hear you say it."

As his right thumb continued its assault on my nipple, his left hand moved down my body. I could barely see straight, let alone form words. My whole body jerked when his fingers grazed over my sex. Our kiss became more intense as he slid two of his fingers inside me.

Reluctantly breaking away from his mouth, I choked out the words he was waiting for. "I want you to fuck me, Ryan. I need you inside me."

I'd never been one for dirty talk or verbalising my desires in the bedroom. Ryan brought out a side of me I never knew existed.

His eyes blazed with satisfaction.

He reached for his wallet and retrieved a condom. I was again privy to his moves as he sheathed himself before pushing into me hard, without hesitation. To say it was overwhelming would be an understatement. As my body adjusted to his size, I realised immediately what I'd been missing with my previous lovers.

Detached from any kind of emotion, I had always enjoyed the physical escape sex brought me. However, this was different; I knew it immediately. When he was inside me, I felt complete. I didn't want to escape. I wanted to experience every single moment.

Tears filled my eyes.

Ryan stopped mid-thrust. "Oh shit, Holly. Are you okay?"

I nodded. Annoyed at my own emotions, I grabbed his firm ass and pushed him deeper into me. "Ryan, please don't stop." I lifted my hips up and wrapped my legs tighter around his waist. "Please don't fucking stop."

Ryan started to move inside me again. My tears quickly evaporated as my whole body was overcome by the rising sensations.

"Harder." I was getting closer and closer to the cliff I so desperately wanted to jump off.

"Come for me, babe."

"Oh. My. God. Ryan!" I closed my eyes as my body shuddered violently. It was the most intense, almost painful, orgasm I'd ever had. It was too much. Ryan Davenport was too much.

"Fuck." Ryan growled into the crook of my neck as I felt him reach his own release. His whole body relaxed on top of mine.

We struggled to return our breathing to normal. After several minutes, he pulled out gently. Propping himself on his side, he stroked my stomach, tracing random patterns around my belly button.

I squeezed my eyes tightly shut and wondered what the hell had just happened between us.

"Hey," he said, breaking into my thoughts. "That was fucking amazing." He leaned over and kissed me tenderly, then got up to dispose of the condom.

I closed my eyes again so I didn't have to see his face when he returned.

"Look at me, Holly."

I forced myself to open my eyes. His gaze was intense.

"Fucking amazing," he repeated.

"Err… Thank you?"

Ryan rolled over onto his back and laughed. "Oh, you are so welcome, Ms Ashton."

I tried really hard not to smile, but it was impossible. Professional mode was way out of context here.

Fatigue overcame me and I yawned. The day had been both emotionally and physically draining. It wasn't late, but I just wanted to sleep.

Ryan pulled me against him so my back was flush against his front. It was beautifully intimate, and I was surprised how much I enjoyed it. He pulled the covers over us so we were cocooned together. I felt safe.

"Go to sleep, Holly." He must have noticed how drowsy I was. He kissed my shoulder and gently stroked my hair.

I drifted off to dream of sapphire eyes and giant chessboards where I was the queen.

Chapter Seventeen

I woke up feeling rested, content and a little sore – in the best kind of way. Ryan had woken me during the night for a repeat performance, which was slower and heart wrenchingly more intimate, as our initial desperation was replaced with a quiet exploration of each other's bodies.

I couldn't get the smug grin off my face as I was flooded with memories from the night before. That lasted for all of about three seconds. Reaching out to his side of the bed, I realised I was alone. The ice-cold fear of regret took hold. Darting my eyes around the room, I located my robe and quickly covered myself up, double knotting the tie for good measure. With no choice but to face him, I made my way down the stairs and was overwhelmed by the delicious smells of bacon and coffee.

"You're awake. I was about to bring you breakfast in bed." His devilish grin disarmed me. I had so quickly jumped to the worst conclusion – clearly, I was expecting him to regret this arrangement.

"I woke up and you weren't there. I, err… didn't know where you were." I couldn't look him in the eye so I stared down at my bare feet, examining the recycled timber floorboards I was standing on.

Glancing up, I could see his upbeat mood had darkened as he stalked towards me. When he was merely inches away, he tilted my chin so I had no choice but to look him in the eye.

"Where did you think I was, Holly? The west wing?"

"I don't know. I guess I thought you'd done a runner. Last night was pretty intense. I thought maybe you'd regretted it."

"Regretted it? You're a crazy woman. Last night was incredible. *You* are incredible." He leaned forward and kissed me hard on the mouth before I had a chance to worry about my morning breath. "Now get your sexy butt back to bed and lose the robe. Breakfast is getting cold."

Needless to say, breakfast went cold. Ryan managed to satisfy me in ways I never knew existed. I barely made it back to bed before I was pounced upon and shown just how wrong I'd been in questioning his mindset.

"Did you really think I'd taken the first seaplane out of here?"

"Maybe?" Blushing, I pushed my face into the pillow until his tickling got so bad I conceded defeat. I was insanely ticklish. Unfortunately for me, exploring my body had revealed this, and now Ryan had the ultimate power over me.

"Stop, please!" I begged him breathlessly. Finally, he showed mercy.

"The first seaplane doesn't leave till lunchtime." He chuckled smugly. "Though I guess I could have stolen a boat."

His teasing earned him a good jab in the ribs, and I half-heartedly tried to break free from his arms.

"Not so fast, sexy, you're not going anywhere."

I resumed my position with my head on his chest and my arm lazily resting across his abs. He stroked my hair and kissed my head.

Much later, we got dressed and spent hours exploring the rest of the idyllic property. Gary arrived to pick us up after lunch. I was genuinely sorry to leave our little bubble.

Chapter Eighteen

We were quiet on the flight home. Ryan held my hand the whole way, his thumb gently tracing my knuckles. I just stared out the window at the changing scenery. As Sydney Harbour came into sight, I felt the tension rise and my stomach drop. By the time we landed, it was unbearable. Ryan tried to take my hand as we walked along the jetty, but I pretended not to notice, rummaging aimlessly in my handbag. Suddenly everything felt different. We were back to reality now. As of tomorrow, he was my client. I had no idea how to deal with that after the night we'd just had.

Just as we reached the end of the jetty, Ryan turned and stopped.

"What's going on, Holly? Talk to me, *please*. I had a feeling you were going to shut down like this." He ran his hands through his hair and looked at the ominous skies.

"Nothing is going on. I'm just tired." The coward in me avoided eye contact.

"Can you drop me home, please?"

"You're going to be the death of me, woman."

We crossed the road and walked back up his parents' street in uncomfortable silence. I kept glancing sideways at him, but he never took his eyes off our destination. Knowing I was entirely responsible for the tension between us was torture. Part of me wanted to leap into his arms, kiss him hard on the mouth and ask where we'd be sleeping that night. But I knew the bubble had burst. We had to face reality.

He drove slowly. The trip seemed to take twice as long as it had the day before. Perhaps that was because it was starting to rain. He pulled up outside my apartment building and cut the engine. The now heavy rain provided welcome background noise. I could feel his piercing gaze on me, and eventually I turned to face him.

"Thanks again for lunch yesterday and for… last night." It felt awkward and stilted, and I really wanted to get the hell out of his car and start building up my walls again.

"Jesus, Holly. Please don't overthink this. We had a great time together. Let's not ruin it now. We've got this completely under control."

I rubbed my forehead with my palm and tried to push my fears aside.

"You're good. I mean… you're right. I'm good." *Shut up, Holly, and get out of the car!*

"This can work. We're on the same page here." He said it with such authority, he almost made me believe it was actually possible. But a feeling deep in my gut knew we were kidding ourselves.

I just nodded.

Glancing out the window, I was surprised to see Jason exiting my building. He appeared angry. I went to open the car door, but Ryan stopped me.

"Wait here." He got out of the car quickly, retrieved an umbrella from the boot, then escorted me to the entrance. Despite the large umbrella, it was impossible to avoid getting wet. Jason was waiting under the awning just outside the building.

"Jason O'Connor, Ryan Davenport." I made the introductions and they shook hands. They greeted one another with professionalism, but I could see the daggers Jason was throwing with his eyes.

"I'll see you later, Holly." Ryan leaned in and gave me a quick peck on the cheek before returning to his car. The Aston Martin roared off, water spraying up in all directions. I watched it disappear around the corner before turning to Jason.

"Hey," I said quietly. I tried to give him a hug. I had no idea what was going on with him, but I had a feeling I was about to find out. He didn't return my hug, which gave me a good indication of his mood.

"Did you sleep with Ryan Davenport?" he asked icily.

"Oh my God, Jase. Really?" My shoulders dropped and I sighed. "Come upstairs and I'll get changed, then let's grab dinner, okay?"

"Are you sure your new boyfriend would be okay with that?"

"He's not my boyfriend. Now do you want to have dinner with me or not?"

"I can't believe I'm going to say this, but no, I don't think I do." Shocked, I watched him walk away. *Shit.*

Hoping to talk to Audrey and Zara, I was disappointed to find Jake mauling Zara on the couch. Ugh… I could hear plates clanging from the kitchen. I found Audrey noisily unstacking the dishwasher, looking less than impressed.

"Can you believe those two?" she asked, roughly shoving the bowls into the cupboard.

"Careful, Aud, those are breakable you know," I suggested bravely.

"They've been at it for hours. I've hinted at them to take it to the bedroom about five times, but they're in a bubble of loved-up horniness. I'm surprised they haven't had sex right there on the couch!"

"Eww, that's my couch," I exclaimed. "I would kill them! Don't worry, I'll take care of it."

I marched back to the living room and grabbed Jake by the collar of his shirt, pulling him off the couch.

"You two. Off my couch. Bedroom or the front door. Your choice."

Jake was clearly startled. Zara just laughed.

"Hey! You're back. How was he?" she asked, winking.

"How was who?" Jake asked.

"Ryan. Sexiest man alive. Remember?" Zara replied.

"Again, thought that was me." Jake nibbled at her neck.

"Seriously, you two. Go to your room! Audrey will be in here with a kitchen knife soon. I'm sparing your lives."

"Okay, okay." Zara held up her hands. "But you have to fill me in later."

"I will, I promise. Now go!"

Once they were safely out of sight, I went back to calm Audrey down.

"Coast is clear." She looked up from the dishwasher. "Lounge room sex situation averted."

"Thanks, Hol. Sorry about my bad mood. I guess I'm a bit

sick of all the lovey-dovey stuff happening around me." She was unable to meet my eyes.

"Fair enough. Do you want to talk about it?"

"Well, you just missed Jason. I don't think he's taking the 'Holly and Ryan situation' very well." She continued her assault on the crockery. Clearly something was really bothering her.

"Did something happen with you and Jason?"

She didn't reply but thankfully stopped unstacking. The glassware was next.

"Tell me what happened," I insisted, touching her arm.

Leaning back against the counter, she stared at her feet. "We slept together last night."

I was a little shocked despite being the one who'd encouraged it. "Oh God. Audrey, that's great! Isn't it?"

"I thought so. But then he asked where you were and when I told him, he wanted to know details. I had to stop him phoning you. I think he was going to beg you to come back! He went totally off the rails." She looked me in the eyes then. "I think we have confirmation that he's in love with you, Holly."

"Shit, Audrey. I'm really sorry he did that to you. I need to sort this out with him. It's never going to happen between us. I thought he knew that."

"Either way, I don't want to be his consolation prize." Tears welled in her eyes, and I hugged her with all the love I felt for her.

"He doesn't deserve you, Audrey. You deserve someone who knows you are the most awesome chick in the world." I pulled back and looked at her so she could see my sincerity. "He's out there, I know it."

"I thought you didn't believe in happy endings." She wiped her eyes and tried to smile.

"Yes, well, you got me there. But I'll make an exception for you. If anyone deserves a happy ending, it's you."

Audrey threw her hands in the air. "I'm over it. It's Saturday night, and I'm standing here sniffling over a man."

"We should go out tonight," I suggested. "How about you call that guy you met at the club last weekend?" I forced myself to sound enthusiastic. As much as I would do anything to help lift her spirits, I'd been kind of hoping for a quiet night in.

"Corey. I guess I could call him to see what he's up to."

"Right. Give him a call while I jump in the shower."

Feeling infinitely better after a hot shower, I ventured out in my towel to find out if I could put on comfy clothes.

When I saw Audrey's giddy smile, I already knew the answer.

"Tonight, we're going north!"

"Okay, great." I feigned excitement.

"Why don't you see if Ryan wants to come? I really enjoyed his company that night we had dinner."

"Okay. I guess I can see if he's up for it."

Ryan replied to my text almost immediately, saying that he would meet us there. He had a few things to take care of first.

Satisfied with my casual yet sexy outfit, I grabbed my journal and started to write. It was cathartic to explore my newfound feelings in my journal, where they could stay safely locked away.

Chapter Nineteen

We ordinarily would have caught the ferry to Manly, but a cab was a much better option in the rain. The cab ride gave me a chance to fill Audrey in on my overnight stay at the Hummingbird. She was beyond thrilled but thought we were crazy for thinking we could keep things casual.

"The chemistry between you two is ridiculous," she'd said, shaking her head.

The bar where we were meeting overlooked the ocean. The palm trees that lined the beachfront were reminiscent of the Hummingbird foreshore. I felt an ache in my heart when I thought of the time I'd spent there with Ryan. There was absolutely no way I could be missing him already. *No freaking way.*

Audrey went in first and I followed her, taking off our coats as we were hit with the warmth from the busy bar. It felt like every male in the room turned to look as we entered. They were no doubt staring at my gorgeous best friend. Whilst I had opted for a casual look, she was rocking skin-tight jeans and a beaded halter top that showed off her slim, toned arms. She never went anywhere in anything but heels, so I was dwarfed by her. I was glad to be out of the limelight – I wanted her to be the centre of attention.

"Audrey! Over here." A good-looking guy fitting Audrey's description of Corey was waving us over.

As we got closer, I could see he was standing with a group of his mates. My eyes locked with the guy standing next to Corey and my blood ran cold. *Sam…*

"You made it," Corey said, pulling Audrey over to him. He kissed her on the cheek, which I thought was sweet. This was just what Audrey needed to boost her self-esteem after the Jason debacle. "These are my friends. Sam, Gavin and Vinny."

Audrey introduced me and we all shook hands. When Sam took my hand, he held on to it as he looked me straight in the eye. Audrey must have recognised Sam, too.

"Oh, Sam. You were at the club last weekend, too." Then she stopped speaking. It must have suddenly dawned on her that I had left with him, making this situation potentially awkward.

"All of us were there," Sam replied, still looking at me. "Holly and I are well acquainted."

"Drinks!" Corey announced. "What are you having, ladies?"

"Bubbles, please," we both replied.

Sam stood close to me. "Busy, huh?" I wasn't quite sure if he was serious or joking.

"Um… Yes, I am busy." I stared at my feet. "I had no idea you were friends with Corey."

"Don't look so stressed out, Holly. We didn't even sleep together." His eyes raked down my body, and his hand gently rubbed my right arm. My body didn't react in the slightest to his touch. "Let me know if you want to hook up again tonight."

"Look, Sam. I did have a good time with you, but I'm here for Audrey tonight. She needs me."

We both looked over at Audrey and Corey. Audrey was in full flirt mode, and Corey was clearly under her spell. He didn't stand a chance.

"Doesn't look like she needs you." Sam smiled and smugly took a sip of his beer.

"I'm… um… kind of seeing someone." I felt awkward saying it because it wasn't completely true. I wasn't in a relationship with Ryan; we were just having casual sex. Sam didn't need to know that though. The truth was, I only wanted to be with Ryan.

"Oh. Okay then. I didn't realise you had a boyfriend."

"Oh no. I'm just doing some work for him. He's not my boyfriend. We're, um…"

Sam raised his eyebrows. "You sure about that?"

Ryan's imposing presence made the hairs on the back of my neck stand on end. His arm came around my shoulders, and I was pulled possessively into his side.

"She's with me."

Sam held his hands up defensively. "Sorry, mate. No harm done. You can't blame a guy for trying." He offered his hand to Ryan, who shook it politely and introduced himself.

"So Ryan," Sam said casually. "Holly here tells me she is working for you. She didn't tell me your company."

"Davenport Property," Ryan replied, a little icily I thought.

"Really? So you're Ryan Davenport then."

Ryan just nodded. He was being rude. Sam was just being friendly and taking an interest.

"Excuse me," Ryan said. He put his beer down and walked off towards the bar.

"Sorry about that," I said. "I'm not really sure what his problem is."

"I'm his problem."

I shifted uneasily. "Well, I'm sorry anyway."

"Don't worry about it." His hand gently rubbed my arm again. "If it doesn't work out with Mr Personality, give me a call. Keen to hook up with you again anytime."

Unfortunately, Ryan returned just in time to overhear that last statement. He looked thunderous.

"Can we go outside for a minute, Holly?" he asked, through gritted teeth.

"Um, okay. Sure." I looked over to Audrey, who had also heard the whole thing.

"You okay, babe?" she mouthed.

I nodded, then followed Ryan outside. We walked in silence across the road and down the steps leading onto the beach. The small waves were gently lapping against the wet sand. Despite the cold, I hungrily breathed in the fresh ocean air. Knowing Ryan wanted to get something off his chest, I looked at him, ignoring the soothing view of the ocean.

"So, what was that about?" I asked, breaking the silence.

"When did you hook up with Sam?" The question seemed to torture him.

I didn't want to lie to him. "Look. I didn't realise he was friends with Corey, or..."

"Or what? You wouldn't have invited me so you could hook up with Sam again?" The hurt in his voice was evident, and I felt a mixture of anger and regret.

"No. I don't want to hook up with Sam again. But I don't see what business it is of yours." I couldn't look at him. Instead, I tried to summon the calming balm of the water.

"Are you serious?" His hands went through his hair in what I was beginning to recognise as his signature act of frustration. "Don't think for a second you're going to be fucking anyone but me, Holly."

"We're not in a relationship. You don't get to tell me what I can and can't do."

"Fuck!" he yelled, making me turn around. "Fuck!" he yelled again, out at the endless expanse of open water.

"What do you want me to say?" Tears welled in my eyes.

After a few deep breaths, he turned and took hold of my hands. "I'm sorry. I didn't like seeing you with him. I didn't like hearing him say he wants to hook up with you again."

"I didn't sleep with him. I don't want to be with him. I don't." I put my arms around his waist and looked up into his tortured face. "This was meant to be just sex, Ryan."

"I know. But I won't share your beautiful body with anyone."

"Fine."

He kissed me, then took my hand, leading me up the beach.

Before we entered, he stopped. "Come home with me tonight."

"Aren't you sick of me yet?"

"Not even close."

Chapter Twenty

"Wow."

"That's one word for it," Ryan chuckled as he nibbled at the dip between my naked breasts.

Ryan lived in a luxurious, serviced apartment on Woolloomooloo Wharf. We'd barely made it through the door when our clothes started hitting the floor, and we stumbled ungracefully towards the bed. There was no talking, no hesitating, no questioning anything other than how quickly we could get naked and he could get inside me. We were like a pair of horny teenagers, each desperate for the release only the other could provide.

When our bodies connected, it was another crazy, intense physical experience. Being completely together was starting to feel more like necessity than desire. When he pulled out of me, I immediately felt the loss. I wrapped my arms firmly around his neck so he couldn't get far. He seemed just as keen to stay wrapped around me.

Eventually, he got up to dispose of the condom. When he returned, he handed me one of his t-shirts. "Will you join me on the deck?"

I got out of bed, pulled his t-shirt over my head, then went to find him outside.

"That's a good look on you." His approving smile made me feel sexy and beautiful. Snuggled under a blanket with Ryan, the outdoor heaters blasting, it didn't matter that I was hardly dressed.

"I think this might just be the perfect arrangement," he said, chinking his champagne glass against mine.

"What?" I scoffed. "You have a little hissy fit and I do whatever you want?"

"Exactly." His cheeky smile made me laugh.

"Don't get used to it, buster."

He kissed me lightly, and I could taste the expensive champagne on his lips. "I think I might already be used to it," he whispered, resting his forehead against mine.

When I put my arms around his neck, my charm bracelet lightly grazed his cheek.

"Tell me about your charm bracelet." He reached back and gently brought my wrist back so he could touch the delicate charms.

"It belonged to my mother. She died when I was fifteen."

I sat back, pulling my hands into my lap, and waited for the anxiety that never came. The words had spilled out before I realised what I was saying. I had just allowed him to know my greatest wound. A man I had only known for a short time. A man I was trying hard to just have casual sex with.

"Oh, Holly, I'm sorry. You didn't talk about her in the past tense in your presentation." He reached for my hands and waited for me to continue.

"I don't usually let my personal life interfere with my career. That was the first time I'd ever mentioned her at work. It was a bit of a shock really."

"Well, I'm honoured. Your presentation was intense, but in a good way. I could tell you were passionate, and I was completely mesmerised. Your colleague, err, Emma?"

"Eva," I corrected with a straight face. I was laughing jubilantly on the inside.

"Oh right, Eva. She clearly has talent, but once you started talking, I was sold."

I felt surprisingly comfortable talking to Ryan about Mum. I opened up further. "My mum was an architect, you know. You may know her designs. Anna Wilson?"

"Are you serious?" He sat up straighter. "She's a legend in the architecture world."

I stared at the incredible harbour view, but my mind was elsewhere. "I didn't mention her name in my presentation because I didn't want it to have any influence." I shook my head and looked him in the eye. "She kept her maiden name for work, so no one ever makes the connection to me."

"You certainly inherited her genius, that's for sure." He leaned forward and kissed me gently on the lips. "I told you my instincts were good."

I would never get tired of looking at him. "Tell me something about your family."

"I thought we weren't getting personal."

"Err… I just told you about my mum. I think you have to tell me something now, to keep things even."

"Fair enough. What do you want to know?"

"How often do you see your sister?"

"Not that often. Aspen lives in Melbourne. Mum flies down regularly to see her, and I catch up with her when I can. I think you'd really like her, actually."

"Aspen is an unusual name."

"It's where my parents met, and most likely where she was conceived, although I'd rather not give that any thought." He scrunched up his face in disgust.

"My mum loved to ski. She would have loved to go to Aspen."

I had so many more questions I wanted to ask about his family, but I was distracted by my growing desire to kiss him again. Ryan looked absent somehow, but I had no idea what he was thinking. Staring at his perfect face, I knew I didn't want anything to ruin this perfect moment.

"Let's go back to bed," I said, snapping him out of his thoughts.

We discarded our clothes on the way back to the bedroom.

"Are you taking birth control?" Ryan asked, as we climbed into bed.

"I am," I replied. "But I've never had sex without a condom."

"I don't want to use them with you anymore."

I looked at him questioningly.

"I want to feel you with no barriers. If we both prove we're clean, would you consider ditching the condoms?"

"Okay," I whispered.

"I won't be having sex with anyone else while our arrangement is in place. And you sure as hell won't be having sex with anyone but me, so—"

I cut him off. "I said okay, Ryan."

"You did? Oh. Okay then."

I was surprised by how easily I had consented to his request. I wanted to feel him without any barriers, too. It was something I'd never experienced before.

He looked at my lips hungrily.

I smiled my consent and Ryan wasted no time grabbing my waist and pulling me against him. Our lips collided, and the ensuing inferno raged once again. Our bodies melded into each other as if they were made to be connected. I was shocked by how quickly I was ready to be taken by him again. The way I felt when we were together was becoming a dangerous addiction.

Despite being content in his arms after making love again, I forced myself to get up and gather my clothes from around the room. My heart wanted to stay, but my head was telling me I was getting attached, and that wasn't good. For this to really work, we needed to keep some boundaries in place.

When I was fully dressed, I turned to Ryan, who was watching me with an unreadable expression.

"Well, um… Thanks?" I said, chuckling awkwardly.

"You are more than welcome," he replied, grinning. "You can stay if you want."

"I think it's best if I go home." I knelt on the bed and kissed him.

He grabbed the front of my t-shirt and deepened the kiss.

"Okay. Okay. I have to go." I pulled away and stood up.

When I reached the door, I glanced back. He was staring at me with that same unreadable expression. Neither of us smiled. We just stared for a few seconds. *What are we doing?*

Chapter Twenty-One

The week passed in a blur of meetings, site visits and more meetings. I was back at the Slater Jenkins offices, so maintaining a professional relationship with Ryan had been no problem. I had only seen him once, and that was at the site with six other people – including Slater. Part of me had hoped for a stolen glance or a warm smile. I got neither. Our arrangement was working.

As I headed home from work on Friday afternoon, my phone alerted me to a text message.

My place or yours?

Once again, we were insatiable the second we were alone in his suite. The more we were together, the more comfortable we became with each other's bodies. Lying naked together, I ran my fingers down his toned abs. A small, raised scar on his lower torso made me sit up for closer inspection.

"What happened there?"

"Oh, that," he replied, sitting up. "Just an old sporting injury." He appeared distracted again. "Are you hungry?"

"Famished. What are you cooking me?"

"Very funny. Let's grab a bite downstairs at one of the wharf restaurants."

We decided on an Asian fusion restaurant and were treated to one of their best tables. I guessed Ryan was a good customer.

"So how was your week, Ms Ashton?" he asked as our dumplings arrived.

"Busy. Lots of meetings and site visits. Yours?"

"You know, I really wanted to come over and kiss you when we were on site together. It nearly killed me to keep my distance."

"Well, that wouldn't have been very discreet." I was happy our arrangement was working so well but was strangely relieved to hear him say he'd wanted to kiss me. I'd sure as hell wanted to kiss him.

"I'd like you to stay tonight," he said, flooring me with his intense gaze.

"You would?"

"I've had a really busy week, and I'd like nothing more than to bury myself deep inside you over and over. I'm not ready to let you go just yet."

His words were both hot and cutting at the same time. He wanted me, but only as a distraction. I had wanted the casual thing, too, but I was starting to feel used.

"I'm not sure that's a good idea." I pushed the remaining dumpling around with my chopsticks.

"Look, Holly. We're keeping our distance during the week. Can't we enjoy each other on the weekends?"

"I guess so."

"Well, that was unconvincing. What's wrong?"

"I know what's going on here, Ryan. I'm not stupid."

"What is it you know, Holly?"

"I know you like me. And I know I like you." I put my chopsticks down and pushed my shoulders back. "I know we are definitely compatible in the bedroom."

Ryan smiled but didn't interrupt.

"I know I've never felt like this about anyone before, and it scares me. It scares me half to death. When I'm with you, I feel alive and beautiful. But none of these things matter because neither of us wants a serious relationship. I'm fairly certain I'm just a useful distraction to you."

"So you think you know a lot then, smarty pants."

I couldn't help smiling at the reference to our first meeting.

"You remember that conversation, don't you?" he asked.

I nodded.

"Look at me, Holly."

I tentatively raised my eyes to his, worried about what was coming.

"I remember it, too," he continued. "I told you there was a sadness in your eyes I didn't understand."

"I remember that. It freaked me out a little."

"Well, something has changed since then. There is still sadness, which I hope you can explain to me properly, but you're happy when you're with me. We were meant to meet, Holly."

I could feel tears welling in my eyes.

"I've had girlfriends, but it's never felt right. My last girlfriend in London wanted to make things more serious, so I broke up with her." He reached across the table and grabbed hold of my hand. "And now I know why it never felt right. She wasn't you."

I was rendered speechless.

"You are drop-dead freaking gorgeous for a start." His thumbs caressed the top of my hands. "I pretty much want to have sex with you constantly. But on top of that, you are intelligent and ambitious. You also have the smartest mouth, a beautiful, creative mind and you make me laugh. The fact that neither of us is desperate to make this more complicated than necessary makes it all the more perfect."

He seemed to know exactly what I needed to hear. We were having a good time. We liked each other but without either of us asking too much. Neither of us wanted a commitment or a future. Perhaps it was the perfect arrangement.

I stayed the night. I stayed for breakfast. I stayed for lunch.

Chapter Twenty-Two

It was Saturday night and I was dressed, ready to go out for dinner. I'd left Ryan straight after lunch and headed home. I'd agreed to go out to dinner with Jason to see if we could sort out our damaged friendship.

"Wine o'clock?' Zara asked, interrupting my thoughts.

"Oh, she lives and breathes."

"Very funny. Jake's taking a shower." She walked into the kitchen and grabbed a bottle of red wine from the rack above the fridge.

"Jason will be here any minute," I called out to her. "I could do with a glass of wine, thanks." *Or maybe a bottle.*

She returned to the lounge room holding two glasses in one hand and the bottle in the other.

Sitting down on the couch next to me, she handed me a glass. "Talk to me, Holly. What's been going on with you this week? I've barely seen you."

"Yes, that's because you've been having crazy, wild sex with Jake. Are you guys officially together now or what?"

"Who knows," she grinned. "We're having fun and we're very compatible, if you know what I mean."

"Ugh. No visuals, thanks."

"So you're giving Jason the chance to redeem himself? How was it working together all week?"

"I'm the ice queen, apparently. We're going out for dinner tonight to try and talk it out. I'm really pissed at him though, Zara. Sleeping with Audrey then going postal about me hanging out with Ryan was completely out of order." I took a sip of wine. "Audrey has forgiven him, but she's the forgiving kind."

"I imagine Corey might have something to do with her forgiving nature?"

"Yep. He's actually a really nice guy from what I can tell."

"So, what made you agree to go out with Jason tonight then?"

"Well, I wasn't going to stay pissed at him forever, especially when he was so quick to apologise to Audrey." His grovelling had been fairly epic. By the end of the week, my frosty demeanour had thawed a little, and Jason saw his chance. "It was actually kind of funny. He looked terrified and approached me with caution. I am a bitch."

"You're not a bitch, Hol."

"It helped that work is going really well. The consultant hired to push my design through council is confident of an approval soon."

"That's awesome, Holly. Your mum would be so proud. And you're not a bitch; you care about your friends is all."

"Thanks, Zar."

"Soooo… what's the deal with Ryan. Are you guys dating?"

"No. We're just 'having sex'," I replied, using air quotes.

"Wow. Okay. Is he okay with that?"

"It was his idea."

"What was whose idea?" Jake asked, appearing from behind the couch, freshly showered.

"Girls' business, sorry." She looked at me and winked.

Jake pulled her up, sat down next to me, then pulled her back down on his lap.

The intercom buzzed. Excellent timing, Jason.

"Doesn't he have a key?" Zara asked. "He never buzzes from downstairs."

"I don't think he's taking any liberties around me for the time being." I stood up and grabbed my handbag. I needed to sort this out. "See you later, lovebirds."

I waved to Zara and Jake as I opened the front door, but they were already completely engrossed in each other. *Ugh.*

When the lift opened, I immediately saw Jason standing in the lobby by the large indoor plant. He appeared awkward and unsure, shifting on his feet. We'd always had such an easy, comfortable friendship. This situation was neither easy nor comfortable, but it was necessary if our friendship had a future.

"Hi," I said, when I reached him.

Without saying anything, he pulled me in for a hug. When I hugged him back, I could feel his whole body relax.

"God, I've missed you, Holly. I'm so sorry about last weekend. Can you forgive me?"

I pulled out of the hug and looked at him. I could see the desperation and sincerity in his eyes. "We need to talk, Jase."

"I know. Let's go."

We walked down to Circular Quay and then to the Rocks. There was a little Italian restaurant there that you could easily miss if you didn't know about it. They made the best gnocchi in the world as far as I was concerned. It was a favourite of ours, and we found ourselves heading there without discussing it.

Giovanni, the owner, greeted us like old friends.

"Buonasera. Good evening Holly e Jason. Benvenuto. Welcome."

"Grazie, Giovanni. Per due?" Jason asked, in perfect Italian.

"Naturalmente. Sempre. Always."

"Grazie." I attempted to use the correct inflection.

He led us through the restaurant and showed us to our table. Once we'd ordered our meals and some Chianti, I knew it was time to get some things off my chest.

"What were you thinking, Jason? Why would you sleep with Audrey if you don't feel that way about her?"

He looked at the red and white tablecloth and didn't reply immediately. I waited for him to speak.

When he finally looked at me, I could see the pain this conversation was inflicting on him.

"I don't know. I wish I could take it back, but I can't."

"Can you tell me what happened? All I know is that you slept with Audrey, found out I was staying overnight with Ryan, then you went a bit crazy."

"We were at Jake's party. Audrey was in a great mood. We were all drinking. She took a call from you and told me you weren't going to make it to the party but didn't tell me why. We kept drinking, which led to dancing, leading to more drinking."

"So you're telling me you were too drunk to know what you were doing?" My anger was rising again, and I was grateful when Giovanni arrived with the Chianti.

"No. That's not what I'm saying. We were fairly drunk, but I remember everything. Audrey is hot. She's an amazing dancer, and I'm definitely attracted to her. We ended up kissing and before we knew it, we were having sex in one of Jake's spare rooms."

"So when did it all go wrong?"

Jason went back to studying the tablecloth.

He started speaking without looking at me. "Afterwards, it occurred to me to ask where you were." He looked up and met my eyes. "I lost my mind, Holly. I couldn't stop thinking about you giving Ryan what I've always wanted from you."

I raised my eyebrows. "A one-night stand?"

"No. That's not what I meant."

"Then what did you mean, Jason? I'd really like to know."

"I knew if you slept with Ryan Davenport, you'd be risking your career. If you were willing to risk your career, that had to mean he'd cracked the Holly Ashton wall of defence. So what's to stop him getting ahold of your heart?"

I was gobsmacked.

"Here you go." Giovanni placed a bowl of gnocchi in front of each of us. The aroma was intoxicating. "*Parmigiano?*"

"*Si, grazie,*" we both said.

The wonderful smell of our meals was not enough to quash the sadness I felt at Jason's admission. Unable to respond, I tucked into my mouth-watering gnocchi. At least the gnocchi was uncomplicated and wasn't asking anything of me.

"Oh my God. This is so good," I said, more to myself than to Jason.

"I pretty much told you I'm in love with you and you're raving about the food." I glanced at Jason's bowl – it hadn't been touched.

I put down my fork and wiped my mouth with my napkin.

"Alright. Let's have this out. I thought I had made it perfectly clear that I don't feel that way about you. I have never led you on. Did you really think I would ever change my mind?"

"Hoped. I think deep down I knew I was deluding myself, but I just hoped you would change your mind once you'd dealt with your mother's death properly. I wanted to be the man you gave yourself to when you were ready."

Suddenly I wasn't hungry anymore.

"What are you talking about?" I was livid. I leant forward and whispered, "I have dealt with my mother's death. I've dealt with it every day for the past ten years. I will have to deal with it every day for the rest of my life. Who the hell do you think you are telling me I haven't dealt with it?"

"Shit, Holly. Don't get angry. We're trying to sort this out, not make it worse."

"Then don't bring my mother into it and don't fuck over my best friend," I snapped.

"I'm sorry." He stared down into his gnocchi.

I took a deep breath. "Look, if it makes you feel better, I don't plan on letting Ryan get a hold of my heart. Happy?"

"No, I'm not happy. Of course I'm not fucking happy. You're my best friend, and I've been in love with you forever. I've made a complete fuck up not only of our friendship, but also my friendship with Audrey. I'm sure I'm not Zara's favourite person either. What part of that do you think would make me happy exactly?"

"I have no idea." I felt drained and confused.

Since meeting Ryan, I felt like I'd jumped out of a plane with no parachute. My friends had always been such a great source of comfort to me. These revelations from Jason were really upsetting.

"Shall we get out of here and go for a walk?" he asked.

"I think that's a great idea. I can't believe you've turned me off my gnocchi. I might never forgive you for that." I managed a smile so he knew I was mostly kidding.

Poor Giovanni looked heartbroken when he saw Jason signalling for the bill, despite the two full bowls of food in front of us.

"Gnocchi no good?" he asked. The poor man looked like we had run over his favourite puppy.

"Oh no," I exclaimed. "Your gnocchi is the best in the world. It's Jason's fault. You should ban him from coming back."

I don't think Giovanni realised I was joking. He glared at Jason, who held up his hands defensively.

"She's kidding. I'm sorry." Jason pretended to tear his hair out.

Giovanni laughed half-heartedly, but he still looked devastated. I wondered if our welcome would be as warm the next time.

We left the restaurant and headed right. George Street wound its way through the buzzing, touristy area of the Rocks and under the southern end of the Harbour Bridge. There were plenty of people around, jostling past us, but we just strolled along, oblivious.

"Are we going to be okay, Holly?" Jason asked, after we'd been walking for a while in silence. "I don't want to lose our friendship. Even if we can never be anything more, I want us to be friends."

"I do, too. But now that you know for sure we'll never be anything more, are you certain you really want to stay friends?"

"I'd be lying if I said I wasn't disappointed, but I'm not going anywhere."

"Okay then. Clean slate? Though I'd like to see you grovelling to Audrey for a while longer."

"Deal. No future for us beyond friendship, no mention of you not dealing with your mum's death, no having sex with our friends, grovel to Audrey."

"I think that covers it." I wanted this conversation to be done. Only time would tell if our relationship really could survive this hurdle, but I was glad we'd had it out. It was time. I loved Jason and I wanted him in my life. I just wasn't *in* love with him.

"Look over there." I pointed across the harbour to Lavender Bay. "That's the Aqua Vue building."

"Wow, that's going to be amazing when the redesign is complete."

"I think so, too." Ryan flashed through my mind. I wanted to be standing there with him. I wanted his arms around me. I missed him. The dull ache in my heart was suddenly replaced with a stabbing sensation. I rubbed my chest frantically.

"What's wrong?" Jason asked, concern etched on his face.

"Nothing. I don't know. My heart hurts. It's okay, it's going away." The pain subsided as quickly as it had come.

"I'll take you home."

"Run tomorrow?" he asked hopefully as we reached my building.

"Sure. I'll meet you at 8?"

"Thanks for tonight, Holly. I'm really glad you were willing to talk after what happened."

"I love you, Jason. I don't throw away friendships easily. But mess with Audrey again and this ice queen might just stay frozen."

"Noted."

"Good night, Jason."

I watched him walk away. Part of me wanted to see Ryan, but I needed some time alone to think through what Jason had said.

When I entered the apartment, Audrey and Corey were cuddled up on the couch watching a movie.

"Hi, guys," I said but kept walking. Audrey would get the hint that I didn't want to stop and chat.

"Night, Hol," she called after me.

I crawled into bed and reached for the wooden box in my bedside drawer. After going years without touching it, suddenly I found myself writing in my journal almost daily.

Ryan had made more than just a small crack in the defensive walls around my heart. He was driving a wedge in. Each time I was with him, the crack deepened. Whenever we were apart, I felt the same ache. However, instead of the pain I thought love would cause, I felt more whole than I had in ten years. I had lied to Jason about not giving Ryan my heart. I was falling in love with him.

As if on cue, my phone alerted me to a text message.

Can I come over? I miss you ;-)

I knew I would have to talk to him sooner or later about how I was feeling, but I wasn't ready just yet. Telling him would mean not seeing him anymore. Instead, I switched my phone off.

Chapter Twenty-Three

Like a coward, I ignored Ryan's many phone calls and text messages the next day. I didn't know what to say. My instincts were telling me to make a clean break. If I didn't end it soon, my career would become collateral damage down the track. That was simply unacceptable. I had worked too hard. However, every time I thought about that conversation, the ache in my chest reminded me I was already in over my head. I was in uncharted territory, and I was terrified.

Audrey and I spent the day in the city. She talked non-stop about Corey and her latest promotion at work. Audrey was a merchandiser for Australia's largest department store chain. We walked through the Queen Victoria Building, and she entertained me by pointing out the flaws in the window displays. She also highlighted the ones she thought were done well and explained why. I loved hearing her talk with such passion and enthusiasm.

"Let's get a coffee," she suggested when she saw me yawning. "Why are you so tired?"

"Um… I didn't sleep that well last night. I have a lot on my mind. I'm fine."

"What's really up, Hol?" she asked, once we were settled at a table overlooking the Town Hall building I loved so much.

I wasn't sure if I was ready to admit that I had feelings for Ryan, so I went with the other unsettling thing on my mind.

"Um… Jason told me he's in love with me."

"Oh." A small laugh escaped from her, but it sounded more like a strangled cat. "So is everything okay with you two then?"

"I think so. I made it crystal clear that our only future is as friends. I think he got the message this time. He does seem really sorry he hurt you."

"I'm not sorry. If he hadn't hurt me, I wouldn't have called Corey." Her smile was tainted by sadness though. "I would always have been second best for Jase."

"Corey seems really great. I'm so glad you met him." I took a sip of coffee and contemplated telling her about Ryan. "I feel like everything is changing lately."

"You can't stop change, Holly. It's inevitable." She shrugged her shoulders and smiled. "Whatever is going on with you and Ryan, you appear happier. I'm seeing glimpses of the Holly I knew a long time ago."

"I don't think I can keep seeing him. I'm in too deep."

"You're falling in love with him, aren't you?" Her smug smile lit up her face.

I couldn't return it.

"Don't fight it, Holly, I'm begging you – open up to him."

"Come on." I stood up and ignored Audrey's eye rolling. "No more boy talk. Let's go."

We spent the rest of the day wandering around the city talking about random crap and laughing endlessly. It was so good to tune out from the noise in my head. When we finally made it back to our apartment late afternoon, Audrey disappeared to get ready to meet Corey for dinner.

I flopped down on the couch and grabbed a magazine from the coffee table. Just as I was ready to zone out completely, Zara appeared from her room and headed straight for the kitchen. She returned to the lounge with a bottle of wine and two glasses.

"Where's lover boy?" I asked, as she handed me my glass.

"We're taking a break," she replied matter of factly.

"What? As in breaking up?" I sputtered my wine.

"No. Why would you automatically assume that? You are such an incredible pessimist."

"Come on, Zara. I'm no expert, but taking a break usually implies breaking up temporarily, doesn't it?"

"We've just had every night together for a while now and thought we'd have a few nights off. There's only so much sex we can have." She sipped her wine, grinning provocatively.

"You are so confusing, Zar."

She raised her eyebrows and scoffed. "Pot. Kettle. Black."

"I'm not confusing. I'm as black and white as they come."

"You're kidding, right?"

"No, of course not." I took a large swig of wine. "Why am I confusing?"

"Oh, I don't know. You're gorgeous, successful and have everything going for you. The hottest man to walk the planet wants you, but you'll ditch him the second it gets serious. Knowing you, you're probably already scheming your exit strategy." She put her glass down and looked me dead in the eye. "You're different since you met Ryan. You're the happiest I've seen you. But you're so hung up on what happened to your mum that you're going to ruin your future with him."

Where the hell did that come from?

"Wow, maybe you should tell me what you really think." My voice was soft and squeaky, and the inevitable lump in my throat took hold.

"I think you need to get over yourself."

"You do, do you?" I stood up, ready to head to the sanctuary of my bedroom.

"That would be right. Walk away and hide. I'm tired of walking on eggshells with you, Holly. You've got to stop assuming what happened to your mum is going to happen to you."

"I'm going to bed." I started walking away, then stopped and turned. "I don't expect you to understand my choices, but I do expect you to respect them. If you don't think you can, I'll move out."

"I'm saying this because I love you. Both Audrey and Jason think the same thing, but Audrey is too close to you and doesn't want to hurt your feelings. Jason probably doesn't want to ruin his chances of marrying you one day."

"And you don't mind hurting my feelings?"

"Nope. I don't want to marry you." She chuckled, then continued seriously. "You need a kick up the butt, Holly. I'm sorry to be the one to do it, but someone has to. You're going to throw something really good away."

Something about the look on Zara's face stopped me from walking out. I returned to the couch and sat down.

"Do you really walk on eggshells around me?" I asked, tentatively.

"All year you pretend to be a pillar of strength when we all know you're still struggling with her death. I just don't know why you think you have to put on this pretence."

"Have you always felt this way?"

"Pretty much. When we were at uni, I asked Audrey about your history. It was obvious you had some sort of baggage. She told me about your mum and how you refused to have a serious relationship so you couldn't consign anyone else to the same fate."

"Look, Zara, I'm sorry if you feel I've been dishonest or deceitful. I just do the best I can. I miss my mum every single day, but I don't want to walk around blubbering about it. I want to get on with my life."

"I get that. But bottling it up for your birthday each year isn't healthy. And even then, you want us to stay away from you. I've never said 'happy birthday' to you, never been out for a birthday drink or bought you a present."

"That's because I don't think of it as my birthday. I think of it as the day I was told my mum was dead." My vision blurred, but I took a deep breath, trying to stop the tears from falling.

"It's still your birthday, Holly. I, for one, think that's something worth celebrating. And your mum's life is something worth celebrating, too. From what Audrey tells me, she was a wonderful lady. I think it's about time you talked to a professional about your grief."

I felt like I'd been simultaneously punched in the stomach and knifed through the heart.

I stood up shakily. "I need to go to bed now. I'm not hiding, I promise. I just need to think things through. Everything is changing too fast."

She nodded and hugged me. Some of the things she'd said were hurtful, but my brain registered truth in her words. My carefully-constructed world was on shaky ground. Somehow I had to find a safe haven before I stumbled into one of the deep crevices opening up around me.

I retreated to my bedroom and instinctively reached for my journal. Holding Mum's charm bracelet in one hand, my journal in the other, Audrey and Zara's words ran through my brain. Both were convinced Ryan was good for me. Perhaps I could let things go on a little bit longer. He could be my safe haven. Was that so selfish? It was his idea in the first place to keep it casual, so perhaps I could let him be the one to end it.

Chapter Twenty-Four

When I arrived at work Monday morning, I was surprised to see Ryan coming out of Slater's office. We locked eyes immediately. He walked towards me, never breaking eye contact.

"You're working from my offices this week." His tone was cold and demanding. "My car is downstairs."

"Um… okay," I stuttered. "I'll just get my things together."

"I'll meet you at our café." The fact that he referred to the café where we'd met as "our café" gave me hope he wasn't too mad at me for ignoring his calls yesterday.

When I walked into the café, he was sitting at the same table where we'd first sat. It was hard to believe that only two weeks had passed since then. So much had happened in that time.

"Hi." I sat down opposite him and picked up my coffee. "Thanks."

"What's going on, Holly?" he asked. "Why have you been ignoring my calls? I was worried." He stared down at his coffee.

"I'm sorry," I replied. "I was confused."

"Confused about what?" He shuffled his seat around so it was closer to mine. "I thought we agreed we had the perfect arrangement."

"I know. We do. I just have a nasty tendency to overthink everything. Ask my friends." I attempted a laugh to lighten the mood. "I'm fine. We're fine."

"Are you sure?" He frowned, looking unconvinced.

"I promise. I'm sorry. I just had to get my head straight."

"Hey." His hand gently took hold of my chin to hold my gaze. "You talk to me when you're overthinking anything. Especially if you're overthinking us, okay?"

"Okay. I'm sorry you were worried."

His hand released my chin. "I thought you were going to end this."

"Nope. You're stuck with me for a while yet I'm afraid."

"I'm not afraid of that, Holly." His relief was clear, and his smile returned.

That one sentence made me wonder if he, too, was getting in deeper than he had anticipated. Maybe we were still on the same page – we'd just moved to the next chapter.

***

A week working at the Davenport offices turned into a month. Our arrangement had been working out perfectly. During the week, we would keep our distance. The project progressed faster than expected, and the mood in the office was upbeat. We hadn't talked again about the status of our relationship.

Ryan rented a new apartment in Milsons Point, overlooking the northern pillars of the Harbour Bridge. Friday afternoons couldn't come soon enough.

"When's your birthday?" he asked out of the blue, as we lay in each other's arms after a particularly athletic workout in the bedroom.

"July twenty-fifth." I hoped he wouldn't remember it was the day we met.

"Oh really? I thought your name might have meant you were a Christmas baby."

"Close." I cringed at the memory. "Dad took Mum for a weekend away to the Blue Mountains. I think they call it a babymoon. She was eight months pregnant with me. They were doing the whole Christmas in July thing, and I decided to enter the world a month early. I was born in the hotel lobby surrounded by Christmas decorations. So they named me Holly."

"Wow. That would have been an unforgettable experience for your parents."

"And the hotel staff, I imagine." I couldn't help laughing.

"Well, it's not your birthday, but I have something for you."

"Really? Why would you get me something?" I felt nervous for some reason.

"Don't freak out, babe," he said, laughing at the shocked look on my face. "It's only very small."

He got out of bed and strode across the room naked. The man was spectacular. He reached into his jacket pocket and retrieved a small, velvet pouch. Turning around, he dazzled me with his smile and the now-unmistakeable look of adoration in his eyes. I was completely in love with him, and I suspected the feeling was mutual. But neither of us was going to say it.

Every time we were apart, I tried to talk myself into breaking it off. But the second I saw him, I was helpless to his magnetic draw. There were no longer crevices in the protective walls I'd built. The crevices had turned into giant canyons, leaving my heart completely vulnerable.

As he handed me the black pouch, my hands started to shake. I slowly untied the drawstring. I could feel something small and hard, and I instantly knew it was a charm. Tears welled in my eyes as I retrieved the tiny piece of silver.

"It's a hummingbird," Ryan whispered.

"I know," I choked, trying to hold on to my threatening tears. "It's beautiful. Thank you." I leaned over and kissed him. "I love it."

"You're welcome, beautiful." He pushed my hair behind my ears and wiped up the tears that had spilled down my cheeks. "I wanted you to have a reminder of me."

"Why would I need a reminder?" I asked, suddenly wary. "I see you all the time."

"I'm heading to London on Sunday for a while. I told you I'd have to meet with investors at some point. The meeting has been scheduled for next week."

"Oh." I took some deep breaths, desperately trying to stop the tears, which continued to fall. "That's okay. I'm sure I can find a replacement while you're away." I don't know why I said it. I think I was trying to conceal my attachment to him.

"What the fuck, Holly?" Suddenly, Ryan was on top of me. "Please don't say things like that. No one touches you but me."

My head was telling me to address this out-of-control situation immediately. When had our "perfect, casual arrangement" turned into an exclusive and jealous relationship? Unfortunately, the rest of my body was enjoying the attention he was paying my breasts. When he started to feather kisses down my stomach, I could barely remember my own name. He always had that effect on me.

"Will you come to a work function with me tomorrow night?" he asked later, when we were almost asleep.

"What?" I asked, groggily. "Do you think that's a good idea, being seen together? We've been lucky so far."

"It's just a construction company putting on drinks. I'm thinking of using them for a future development. It would be much more bearable if you came. No one from Slater Jenkins will be there."

"Okay. I don't see the harm." Famous last words.

Chapter Twenty-Five

I couldn't stop thinking about Ryan's outburst the night before. It might have been just a knee-jerk reaction to my joke about replacing him, but something about it bothered me.

Knowing he was leaving for London the next day, I decided to just let it go. Perhaps some space was exactly what we needed.

"Let's have lunch at Watsons Bay today," Ryan suggested as we walked down the street to get a coffee. "It's a perfect day to sit outside. Invite your friends if you like. I'll see if Mark and Toby are free."

I had met his best mates from school a few times and really liked them.

"Okay, I'll give Audrey a call."

Audrey was keen – and she was bringing Corey, Zara and Jason, too. Zara had broken up with Jake a few weeks ago. She appeared unfazed, as far as I could tell.

"I'll pop in to see Mum and Dad quickly if that's okay? It's on our way, and I haven't seen them in ages."

"Sure. Okay." I hadn't been back to their place since the morning we flew to the Hummingbird. "I haven't met your mum."

"I have to warn you: Mum and Dad can be a bit hard to take when you get them together. I apologise in advance for their behaviour. It's just their way."

Ryan parked the Aston in the visitor's parking spot, and we walked hand in hand into the luxury apartment building.

Ryan's mother looked shocked, possibly even horrified, to see us. "What are you doing here, Ryan?" She was still tying her pink robe around her waist. I thought that was odd, given it was nearly lunchtime.

"Good to see you, too, Mother," Ryan replied sarcastically.

"Oh, sorry, son. How are you?" She gave him a kiss on the cheek but was clearly agitated by his presence.

"I'm good. Mum, this is Holly Ashton. Holly, this is my mother, Jessica Davenport."

"Nice to meet you, Mrs Davenport," I said politely.

"Oh good God, girl. Call me Jessica."

"Okay. Jessica." I laughed a little. There was something about her I liked immediately.

Jessica glanced behind her. "How about I get dressed and we pop out for a coffee?"

Ryan stepped past her. "What's going on, Mum? I thought you'd be happy to see me."

"Of course I'm happy to see you, darling. I'm just a bit tied up at the moment." Her cheeks flamed.

I was struck by the horrible thought that we'd interrupted his parents having sex.

"Who's at the door?" a man's voice called out from another room.

The flush on Jessica's cheeks drained, and she suddenly looked pale.

"Who is that?" Ryan asked in barely more than a strained whisper. "That's not Dad's voice. Are you having an affair?"

Jessica's lack of response was all the confirmation required.

"Oh my God. You're having an affair." Ryan started pacing the room, looking disoriented.

I just stood in the doorway like a deer in headlights. I had braced myself for some discomfort, but this was out of the ballpark.

"You should've called," Jessica replied, eventually.

"Why? So you could've hidden this from me?"

Snapping out of my stupor, I moved to stand next to Ryan. He seemed oblivious to my existence, but that was understandable.

He picked up a frame off the bookshelf next to us. It was his parents' wedding photo.

"Yes. That's exactly why. This is none of your business, Ryan."

"My mother having an affair behind my father's back is none of my business?" he seethed.

"Your father knows. We are getting a divorce. He's been seeing other women for years."

The frame dropped out of Ryan's hands and crashed to the hardwood floor. All I could do was stare at the photo, now covered with shattered glass.

"I heard a crash. Is everything okay?" The man whose voice we'd heard appeared in the lounge room. Well, this was awkward.

"Please, Jonathan. This isn't the time for introductions," Jessica said.

Jonathan looked at Ryan, then at me, before disappearing back to the bedroom.

I stepped forward and grabbed Ryan's hand, squeezing it gently. He didn't say anything. He didn't move. He just kept staring at the closed bedroom door. I thought maybe he was in shock.

Jessica grabbed a dustpan and brush and started nervously cleaning up the mess. I just stared at her, trying desperately to work out the best way to handle this.

"I'm really sorry, darling," she said, glancing up. "But it's been a long time coming, and it's for the best."

"How could you do this? And where the hell is Dad?"

"He hasn't lived here for a long time, Ryan."

"What are you talking about? I visited him here a couple of months ago."

"He's not meant to be here, but he turns up from time to time when he's had a few too many drinks. I don't have the heart to take his key."

"I need to leave," Ryan whispered, more to himself than to his mother. "I have a plane to catch tomorrow. Jonathan seems really great."

I could hear the sarcasm dripping off his last comment.

He strode towards the door, dragging me behind him. I managed to glance back and mouth a rushed goodbye.

We sat in the car in silence for a long time. When I couldn't take it any longer, I spoke quietly. "Do you want to go home? I can just call the guys and tell them something came up."

He didn't look at me, but he nodded his head a fraction.

I called Audrey, then used Ryan's phone to call Toby. There was no way Ryan could be social right now.

We drove in silence all the way back to my apartment. I

wasn't sure what he needed from me – if he needed anything at all.

"Do you want to come up?" I asked, when he didn't make a move to get out of the car.

"I need some time to think, Holly." He looked at me, and I was shocked by the hurt in his eyes. He was crushed. "I'd like to be alone." He turned his gaze back to the windscreen.

"Okay. Whatever you need. I presume we won't be going to the function tonight?"

"No. I need to go. You don't have to come if you don't want to."

"I'll come." I reached over and kissed his cheek. He flinched at my touch. "See you later, then." As I started opening the door, he grabbed my arm.

"Wait. I'm sorry about all of this, Holly. I'll pick you up at seven, okay?"

"Don't be sorry. I can't imagine what you're going through right now, but I know how consuming grief can be." I kissed him again, on the lips this time. He returned my kiss briefly, then squeezed his eyes shut and pulled back.

"I'll see you later."

As I watched him roar off, it occurred to me that I'd never really pushed him to explain why he was so averse to serious relationships. Today's drama would no doubt be the last nail in the coffin for him. I guess we were both as screwed up as each other.

Chapter Twenty-Six

"You look stunning," Ryan said as I walked out of my apartment building.

I had put Audrey in charge of my outfit, and judging by Ryan's lustful stare, she had met the brief. She had talked me into a short, black, satin dress with shoestring straps and silver detailing. It was sexy, yet elegant. I knew Ryan would love it. She had also insisted I complete the outfit with her silver, strappy Jimmy Choos. I left my hair out and wore a little more makeup than usual. Ryan was hurting, and I didn't know how to help him. But I did know how to distract him.

"You don't look so bad yourself," I replied as I approached.

"Let's just skip the drinks and head back to my place." He kissed me with an urgency that I suspected had more to do with today's events than with me.

"I'm all dressed up now, and you did say it was important."

"You're right," he groaned. "Let's go."

The drinks were at an upmarket bar at the King Street Wharf. It was a beautiful evening, and it should have been a great night. Unfortunately, Ryan was beyond tense, and our usually-easy conversation was stilted and awkward.

"So which construction company did you say it was?" I asked, as we were about to enter the bar.

"Tresswells."

I stopped in my tracks. *Sam. Bloody hell.*

"What's wrong?" Ryan asked when I didn't move.

"Oh. Nothing. My shoes are hurting." I didn't want to go in, but I couldn't just stand outside.

"Come on." He took my hand and led me towards the door. "I'll find you a seat or a bar stool, okay?"

We walked in, and I glanced around nervously. *No Sam.* Maybe I was worrying for no reason. I just didn't want to upset Ryan any more when he was already fragile.

As Ryan headed for the bar, I perched on a bar stool with my back to the front door, scanning the room. "Here you go." Ryan handed me a glass of champagne.

"Thanks. I'm okay here if you need to go do your thing."

"Okay. There are a few people I need to talk to. I won't leave you for long. Come and join me if you want."

I grabbed him by the tie and kissed him. "I'm fine. Don't worry about me." I couldn't wait to get out of there so we could be alone.

I let go of his tie, and he sauntered off towards a group of executives. I watched him transform into a powerful businessman. Hours earlier, I'd witnessed this same man crushed and vulnerable. It hurt to remember the look in his eyes when he'd realised what was going on.

"Holly?"

My body went cold. I swivelled around to come face-to-face with Sam.

"Sam. Hi. Good to see you again," I lied through gritted teeth, glancing over at Ryan. Sam really needed to disappear before he returned.

"Don't stress, Holly." Sam's eyes took in my dress. "I didn't realise you'd be here." He cocked his head towards Ryan, who was still talking to the Tresswell execs. "Still got a boyfriend, I see."

"Um… Yes… I guess I do." Ryan and I could no longer pretend our relationship was casual, and I certainly didn't want to lead Sam on in any way.

"You *guess* you do?" Sam asked, smirking. Sipping his beer, he appeared to enjoy watching me squirm as he took a step towards me.

I needed to get rid of him before Ryan saw us together.

"Look, Sam." I placed my hand on his chest and pushed gently to keep him from coming any closer. "I can't talk to you right now, okay?"

I sensed Ryan's presence behind me, and I took a couple of quick gulps of my champagne. It helped a little.

"You okay?" he asked me, completely ignoring Sam.

I nodded as Sam took a step back.

"I can't be here right now." His whispered voice was cold and foreign. "I'm going home."

I jumped down from my stool. "Okay, let's go."

"You sure you don't want to stay here with your fuck buddy?"

Ouch!

"I'm going to pretend you didn't just say that to me." I grabbed his hand. "Let's get out of here."

"You know where I live, Holly," Sam said, snidely.

Ryan snapped around to face him. "You keep your hands off her. Do you understand me?"

"Fuck off, Ryan."

My eyes flicked to Ryan. The look of sheer rage on his face was confronting. With clenched fists, he moved in front of me, blocking my view of Sam.

"It's not worth it, babe," I said, grabbing his arm. "Let's go."

Ryan's whole body was tense. Sam looked nervous but stood his ground. They faced off, neither one moving.

Stepping between them, I pushed gently on Ryan's chest. "Don't make a scene in front of everyone. Let's go outside."

Ryan's shoulders dropped, and he ran his hands through his hair. Without saying a word, he turned and started walking towards the exit. I glared at Sam, then followed after him.

We walked in silence onto the edge of the boardwalk. A ferry was coming in to the dock to our left, and I felt a pang of envy watching the carefree tourists jostling to get off.

"I don't know if I can do this, Holly." His hands went through his hair again. "I'm living my own private hell, and you're in there flirting. Maybe *he* can be my replacement while I'm in London." His voice had that same cold tone.

I started walking away from him. He had no right to talk to me that way. Then I remembered the hurt in his eyes earlier that day, and I turned back.

"What do you want me to say?" Tears welled in my eyes.

"I love you, Holly." He said it so quietly, I wasn't even sure I'd heard him correctly.

"What?" I took a step closer.

He looked at me and shrugged. "I love you, and I know you love me, too."

It may have been the glass of bubbles I drank too quickly, but

I felt a heady mix of nausea and elation.

"What happened to our 'perfect casual arrangement'?" I asked, a little sarcastically. I took another step, until I was standing just out of reach.

"I think we both know it's always been more than that." He looked at me, and his usually warm, sapphire eyes appeared more like coal. "The problem is I just don't think it's enough. I tell you I love you, and you deflect. Last night when I told you I was leaving, you joked about replacing me." He attempted a smile, but it didn't come close to reaching his eyes. "We'll just end up hurting each other."

I felt like he'd stabbed me through the heart. Despite knowing we had an expiry date, the reality hurt so much more than I could have anticipated.

I stood up straight and pushed my shoulders back. "I don't understand where that leaves us." I didn't even try to hold back the tears that rolled freely down my cheeks.

Instead of wiping them away, he turned and stared out at the water. Boats of all shapes and sizes dotted the view. "I leave tomorrow, so we'll have some space from each other for a while. Perhaps that'll help."

"This feels a lot like an ending." I could barely speak through the enormous lump in my throat.

He turned back and cupped my face in his hands. "We need to let each other go. I can't deal with this now. I thought I could. But seeing you with Sam –" He shuddered. "Seeing you with Sam after what happened today with my mum? Well, let's just say I'm a bit fucked up right now, and that just pushed me over the edge."

"Let's just make it a clean break then." I felt my walls reforming. "This is all I can ever be."

"Jesus Christ, Holly. Are you serious? I'm not going to give up on us. If I can clear my head and reconcile this shit with my parents, if you can sort out your aversion to relationships, perhaps I can win you back one day."

"I'm not some trophy." I barely knew what I was saying through my foggy haze. "Being with me is not winning."

He held my hands. "I realise you're not a trophy. I've never seen you like that, and I've certainly never treated you like that. It's just the wrong time for us."

Every atom of my body wanted to give myself to this man completely. I had no idea what was enabling me to stand strong and not beg him to reconsider. He looked at me with such intensity, I had to break eye contact for fear of disintegrating into a pool of tears.

I knew about grief and I knew about pain. This inevitable ending to our attempted relationship cut a new wound in my already-broken heart.

"Can we spend tonight together?" I asked. I wasn't going to beg, but I needed closure. I needed to feel completed by him one last time.

Ryan nodded without meeting my eyes. While he went inside to say his goodbyes, I remained where I was. There was no way I was going to risk seeing Sam again.

We returned to my apartment in silence. Neither of us knew what to say. It was devastating.

Thankfully, Audrey and Zara were out. We went straight to my bedroom and undressed quietly. We had spent so many nights together, but this felt completely different. Perhaps, knowing it was the last time, we didn't want to rush it.

We climbed into bed, but made no move to touch each other.

Ryan spoke first. He looked at me with such pain in his eyes. "We need to save ourselves from our own demons. We both have a lot to work through if we have any chance of a future down the track."

Tears were running freely down my face as I looked at this sweet, beautiful man. Ryan pulled me to him, and as we lay on the bed, skin to skin, gazing at each other, my heart broke just a little bit more as I considered what might have been. I needed to make him understand so he could let me go.

"I can't save myself from something I have no control over." I paused to make sure he was taking in my words. "I can only control who is affected. I'm a ticking time bomb, and anyone who gets close will be collateral damage." I paused again to allow him to process what I was saying. I couldn't resist touching his face. "You have no idea what my family has gone through. I know you are in hell at the moment, but I've been in hell for ten years. I don't want a serious relationship because I've seen the destruction of a man. Of a family. I choose not to inflict that on anyone. That's my choice."

Ryan grabbed my hands and held them. "You can't be serious."

He needed to understand now that I was taking "one day" off the table. "I'm deadly serious. My mother died from the same thing that took her mother's life at the same age. It's in my DNA. This stops with me. I've made my choices and I can live with them. I was horribly selfish letting this go so far, but I just couldn't stay away from you. It's never been this hard to keep my distance. It will be easier when you're in London."

"You're making a terrible mistake. You're not selfish, you beautiful, crazy girl." He stroked my hair and kissed me lightly on the lips. "You are selfless beyond comprehension. But I don't accept it. You deserve to be happy, Holly. I hope one day I can be the one to make you happy." He closed his eyes for a moment. "I can't even think about you being with anyone else."

"Can we not talk about this anymore?" I asked. "I'm exhausted. I want to spend tonight with you. I want to pretend this is uncomplicated. Can we do that for one more night?"

"Do me a favour?"

"What's that?"

"Don't go running to Sam or some other asshole until we've both had some time to think, okay? I want you to be mine. I do."

"That's the thing, Ryan. I'm not anybody's… ever. I don't want to belong to someone. My mum and dad belonged to each other, and now Dad is forever damaged. You can't imagine what it's like to watch both your parents die."

"What do you mean? Your dad's still here."

"He died the second she stopped breathing. I won't do that to someone. I absolutely won't do that to you. Nothing you say will change my mind. If you want me tonight, I'm yours. But tomorrow we need to let each other go."

The look on Ryan's face was heartbreaking. I could see the hopelessness of our situation dawn on his perfect features. Neither of us said another word. There was nothing left to say.

We made love with a passion I didn't know I was capable of, allowing our bodies to convey the words that were too painful to speak. We spoke to each other through our kisses, through our caresses, through the joining of our bodies. As he kissed his way down my naked body, I heard his heart speaking the words I desperately wanted to hear.

When I felt his body relax and his breathing even out, I whispered the words I'd never been able to say. "I love you, Ryan."

When I woke up the next morning, he was gone. The devastation pushed me into a dark hole, and I wasn't certain I could find my way out.

Chapter Twenty-Seven

"Holly. Can I come in?" I could hear Audrey whispering from outside my bedroom door. "It's nearly lunchtime. Are you going to get up?"

"Come in," I croaked. I had been crying for hours and felt groggy and hungover despite having had only one glass of champagne. I was emotionally drained. My defensive walls had been shattered beyond repair.

"Oh, Hol, I'm so sorry." She climbed onto my bed and enveloped me in a comforting hug. "Ryan called from the airport asking me to check on you. He didn't tell me what happened, but I'm guessing it wasn't good." She let me go and sat cross-legged on my bed. "Tell me everything."

"We ended it." I started sobbing again as soon as I said it aloud. "It was a mutual decision. It's for the best."

"I don't think you can convince yourself of that bullshit, so don't bother trying to convince me 'cause I'm not buying." She handed me a tissue. "I'm going to need more info."

I tried to explain what had gone so wrong in such a short space of time. Recounting the scene at his parents' apartment, then describing how we'd run into Sam and our horrible conversation outside the bar, I felt nauseous. If we had just driven straight to Watson's Bay yesterday for lunch instead of stopping, he'd still be going to London, but we wouldn't have ended things with such finality. I knew we weren't a forever deal. I knew it was going to end one way or another. I'd just hoped we could keep things as they were for a bit longer.

Love just wasn't the right path for me. I loved my mum more than life itself, and she was taken from me. Despite my best efforts to avoid it, I had fallen in love with Ryan, and now he was gone, too.

"I'm done, Audrey. I'm going to wallow in self-pity for a while, then I'm going to pick myself up. Breathe in. Breathe out. One foot in front of the other." I looked her dead in the eyes. "I can get through this. This is what I do."

"Look, Hol, can you do something for me?"

"Of course. Anything."

"Go and see your dad before you shut yourself off completely again. Ask him how he's doing."

"Why would I do that?"

"You need to talk to him about your mother. You need to hear his side of the story. It's way beyond freaking time."

"What do you mean? I know his side of the story. Mum was the love of his life and she died. The end."

"Just go and see him, Holly. I'm serious about this."

*****

The next morning, I called Slater, who agreed to my request for a day off. There was no way I could face work or risk hearing Ryan's name. I needed a day to compose myself.

Next, I called my dad and arranged to visit him later that morning.

Without giving it much thought, I drove the long way. It was a route I usually avoided because it went past the hospital where Mum died. I pulled over and stared at the foreboding, brown building. If a building was a person, this one would be mean and sinister, imposing death and destruction on all in their path.

Zara's words from the other night ran through my mind.

You are such an incredible pessimist.

Zara was right. I saw things with such certainty. Relationships are doomed, hospitals are places of death. I'm going to die young, and everyone around me will be collateral damage. No rainbows and butterflies here!

I put the car in drive and headed north up the highway with new determination.

***

"Is everything okay?" Dad asked, as we sat down on the back verandah with a cup of tea.

"Not really, no." I looked at him, expecting to see horror or at least concern. Instead, he smiled.

"Talk to me, Holly. And I don't mean about the weather. Just talk to me."

I felt a weight I didn't even know I'd been carrying lift from my shoulders.

"I think I'm falling apart, Dad." Tears immediately blurred my vision. "I miss my mum."

"I miss her, too, sweetheart. Every day." His eyes were misting. It broke my heart.

"I'm sorry. I didn't mean to upset you. This is why I haven't talked to you before about this. You've been through enough. I wanted to be strong for you."

"Oh my God, Holly. Is that really the reason? I thought you were handling it so well. I thought you had moved on. I guess I thought the fact you followed in her footsteps as an architect must have really helped you."

"It does help me in some ways. It helps me remember her." I wiped my eyes, and Dad passed me a tissue. "It helps me remember the good times, when she was strong and taught me how to look at the world. My success is because of her."

"But you're still falling apart."

"I was there, Dad. I know I was only fifteen when she died, but I remember it like it was yesterday." I swallowed a few times before continuing. "I remember the look on your face when you told me it was time to go to the hospital. I don't remember her voice at all, but I remember *your* voice telling us to say goodbye to her in that horribly small hospital room. And I remember realising that a big part of you had died with her."

A single tear trickled down my father's face, but he was smiling. *Why is he smiling?*

"It's true, my darling girl. Your mother was the love of my life. There was no one before her, and there will be no one after her. She was my sun, my moon, my heart and soul. She was my everything."

"Then why are you smiling?" I asked incredulously. "How are you even functioning?"

"Because for eighteen incredible years, I had everything." His smile grew larger. "Some people never get that – I got eighteen years. Of course I wanted more. I wanted my forever. But I was lucky to get any time at all with that woman." He walked over to my chair. Squatting down beside me, he reached out and held my hand. "Plus, she gave me you and your sisters." He placed his other hand over his heart. "She's still here with me, Holly. I'm not just functioning. I'm living."

"But if you'd never met her, you wouldn't have had to watch her die."

"It was worth it. It was so much more than worth it, I can't put it into words. You'll understand one day, when you meet that person who changes everything."

My thoughts immediately went to Ryan. Even though I knew what we felt for each other was life altering, I'd still told him there was no hope for us.

"I think I already have," I whispered. "But I've thrown it away."

Dad stood and pulled me to my feet. "Let's go inside. I want to show you something."

He led me towards the one room I hadn't set foot in for ten years – their bedroom. As we reached the door, I stopped.

"I can't go in there."

Dad took my hand reassuringly. "You need to."

I took one tentative step forward, then another. As we walked through the door, I closed my eyes. My other senses went into overdrive, trying to find links to this once-familiar environment. Mum had always kept fresh flowers in their room. She didn't have a favourite so there was no one particular perfume reminiscent of her, but she loved jasmine, and that's what I could smell.

Opening my eyes, the first thing I saw was a glorious bunch of jasmine in a vase by the window.

"The smell reminds me of her," Dad said when he saw me staring at the arrangement.

"I remember." I smiled and managed not to cry.

As I looked around, the horror I had associated with this room was replaced by happy memories. I remembered her getting dressed for one of her work functions and letting me choose her jewellery. I remembered helping April make our parents breakfast in bed on their birthdays. I remembered them letting me sleep in their bed when I had nightmares. This had been a safe and happy place for me, and I had forgotten that.

Dad reached up to the bookshelf and took down a photo album I'd never seen before.

"This is an album your mum made before she got sick the second time." He handed it to me. I sat down on the bed and carefully opened it.

The photos at the beginning of the album had been taken in London. I'd seen the one of Mum and Dad in Hyde Park kicking up their heels. It was a happy photo. I couldn't help smiling at the young couple holding hands, completely carefree.

"I love this photo." I ran my finger over it reverently.

Dad sat down next to me and turned to the next page. There were photos I'd never seen before of Mum and Dad with people I didn't recognise.

"Did your mum ever tell you how we met?"

"Yes. She said you were at a party at one of her friend's houses in Hammersmith when you were living in London."

"That's right. She was at teaching college, and I'd been

transferred to London for work. I didn't even want to go to the party, but my flatmate begged me to be his wingman. He fancied one of the girls who was going to be there."

I'd never heard the details of their meeting and I was riveted.

"I walked into the small flat and immediately saw the most beautiful woman I'd ever laid eyes on sitting on the other side of the room. Her leg was in a cast, and she looked miserable. I was drawn to her immediately. She was so far beyond beautiful. Ordinarily, I would've been intimidated, but there was something about her that made me walk over and introduce myself."

I'd never heard my dad speak so openly about Mum before and I wondered if he'd been waiting for me to open up to him all these years.

"What happened next?" I asked, suddenly craving every detail. "Did you ask her out?"

"Not immediately." He shook his head and chuckled. "She pulled out a cigarette and asked for a light."

"Seriously? You hate smokers." I was shocked that he would be interested in someone who smoked.

"Honestly, Holly, she could have injected heroin into her eyeballs and I still would've been completely smitten."

"Wow. That is… really romantic. I had no idea. I wish I'd talked to you about her more after she died."

He put his arm around my shoulders. "I think both of us could have benefited from sharing our grief instead of bottling it up. I should've asked you how you were doing. I shouldn't have let you ignore your own birthday. I've let you down."

Turning to face him, I looked him in the eyes. "No, Dad.

You haven't let me down. I didn't want to celebrate my birthday because I didn't want you to pretend to be happy on the anniversary of her death." I rubbed my forehead. "*I* didn't want to pretend to be happy on such a sad day."

"I wouldn't have been pretending. I'll always be happy you and your sisters were born. I love you all so much."

"I love you, too. I'm sorry I've been so distant. I just found it so hard to talk to you about her initially. You always got that desperately sad, vacant look, and I felt like having me around made it harder for you."

Dad shook his head. "April reprimands me regularly about that look. I don't even realise I'm doing it until she snaps me out of it. I'm not sad, though."

"Really? You look like you've lost the will to live when you space out like that. It made me so sad, and I thought I was the cause. So I stayed away more and more. I wanted to be strong for you, April and Jamie, but I couldn't do it. I was weak." I looked down at the photos of my vibrant and beautiful mother. "I *am* weak."

"When I space out like that, I am re-living one of the millions of happy memories I have of your mother or you girls. I'm in my happy place." He tapped the side of his head. "I have a lifetime of happiness stored up here that I can go to anytime I want. That's enough for me."

Dad took the album and opened it to a photo towards the end. It was a close-up of Mum's beautiful face. "I know you've suffered because of what happened at the end of her life. But you have to know she was a fighter. She never gave up, and she fought until her body was spent. I'll always remember her as the strongest woman I've ever known. That fight lives on in you." He gently touched the photo, as if he was caressing her face. "Don't let your chance slip away. If you can find what your mother and I had, it's worth the risk."

My whole world turned on its axis. *Worth the risk.*

"Do you want to know what I miss most about her?" he asked.

"Of course I do," I choked out, my eyes blurry.

"I miss talking to her."

I nodded in agreement. That was the exact same thing that I missed most about her.

"You can be compatible with someone and have a really good life," he continued. "But it's a special connection when you're on the same page on all the important things. We could talk to each other about anything and everything with no judgement or criticism. We never had to work at our marriage." He looked at me and smiled. "It was just… easy. I want that for you three girls." He continued looking through the album, smiling at the photos. "I want you to find your same-page person."

"Wow, Dad. I've been so wrong about so many things. I'm not exactly sure what to do with myself."

"Wait here a second." He walked out of the room. I sat on the bed and stared out the window to the back garden. When he returned, he handed me a business card.

"What's this?" I flipped the card over to see a woman's name followed by a bunch of letters.

"She's a grief counsellor."

"I don't know, Dad. I've heard so many horror stories."

"Me too. This woman is a professional, and she's really

helped me. For years after your mum died, I did little more than exist. I got out of bed each day and put one foot in front of the other because April and Jamie still needed me. About a year ago, Sophie, one of your mum's friends, suggested I speak to this woman. I guess she saw through my pretence." He pointed to the card in my hands. "I'm not going to lie and say it made everything okay. Nothing will ever make it okay. But it helped to talk to someone objective in absolute confidence."

He walked over to the window and looked out in silence for what felt like a long time. When he turned back, his eyes were bleary. Sitting back down, he put his arm around my shoulders. "She asked about how my daughters were coping. I realise now the answer I gave her was just wishful thinking on my part. I'm so sorry, Holly."

"Don't be sorry, Dad. I've been surrounded by wonderful friends and family the whole time. But I'm starting to think maybe I need this." I sobbed onto my father's shoulder for a long time.

What had I been doing for the past ten years? I'd made some monumental assumptions about something I really didn't understand. I thought Dad's life had essentially ended when Mum died, that he had nothing left to live for. I was wrong.

We hugged and cried, then we cried some more. It was the most beautifully cathartic experience I'd ever had.

When I had cried myself dry, we went back to the kitchen and made tea.

"So, tell me about the lucky guy," Dad said, handing me a mug.

"Oh, um… Well, his name is Ryan. He's a property developer.

He chose my design for his latest project." I looked up at the wall where a cluster of frames showcased some of Mum's favourite buildings from around the world. I noticed there were several additional frames – the most famous of Mum's designs. Dad must have added them. I smiled. "He's a big fan of Mum's work."

"So he has excellent taste then."

"We're not on the same page, though. It was just too complicated." I sipped my tea and looked away, trying to hide my awkwardness.

"You don't really want to talk about this with your father, do you?"

I rubbed my forehead, wondering how to respond. Dad laughed.

"Still have that habit, I see."

"What do you mean?" I looked at him curiously.

"Your mum did it, too. As a child, whenever you were nervous or overthinking something, you would rub your forehead. I was often worried you were going to draw blood. Anna did it a lot when she was working on her designs. You must have picked it up from her."

"I didn't know that."

"You are a lot like her, you know. April and Jamie look more like her than you do, but you are the most like her in other ways. In the ways you can't see." His look changed slightly. "There was a fire in you, Holly. Perhaps if you talk to someone, they'll help you find it again."

"I don't think I've ever let anyone try to help me. I thought I had it all under control. I'm starting to realise I've been wrong about everything. It's surprising I have any friends left."

"You're still you, and you're stronger than you give yourself credit for. You're a beautiful, caring and special person, just like your mum was. The people worth knowing recognise that in you. It's your job to find yourself again so you can have *your* everything. I want that for you, my darling." He hugged me and whispered in my ear. "Find your fire again, Holly."

Several cups of tea later, I left Dad's house feeling a spark of warmth deep in my stomach.

On the way home, I stopped in front of the hospital again. This time, as I looked up at it, I tried to stop my mind from immediately gravitating to the associated trauma. Instead, I remembered Audrey spending a night there when we were about eight years old. She was having her tonsils out. She had been so excited that jelly and ice cream were on the menu for her. She loved all the attention she got from the nursing staff.

I then looked beyond the big brown building to the smaller cream one – the maternity hospital. I was ten when Jamie was born, so my memories were more than just snapshots. Mum looked tired but happy as she gazed at her wrinkly baby. I remember I thought it was strange that her head was cone-shaped and her skin was purple. Dad had struggled to reassure me that she was perfectly normal. I smiled at the memory.

In front of the hospital was a perfectly-manicured cricket oval. There weren't any games being played, but a few kids were kicking a ball around in the sunshine. I was starting to notice the good things.

Rummaging around in my handbag, I pulled out the card Dad had given me. Without overthinking it, I dialled the number and made an appointment.

***

The night after my second session, a few weeks later, I pulled out the letter my grief counsellor had suggested I write to Mum. She'd explained that directing my words to the person for whom I was grieving could be a useful tool in expressing and understanding my thoughts. I also read the poem I'd written for her funeral, and I realised how far I'd come.

Chapter Twenty-Eight

Three months later

"Merry Christmas!" Audrey, Zara, Jason and I chinked our champagne glasses.

"I know you'll all be getting turkey and ham over the next few days with your families, so I've gone for a vegetarian dish. Giovanni taught me how to make it." I placed four bowls of gnocchi down and took my seat at the round table. "I've been slaving away in the kitchen, and I expect some over-the-top appreciation for my efforts."

"Since when are you besties with Giovanni?" Jason asked a little dejectedly. "I still can't look at a bowl of gnocchi without cringing."

"He runs a cooking class once a month at the restaurant. This is his recipe – sage, truffle and kale with homemade gnocchi pillows of goodness."

"Did you seriously make the gnocchi? It smells divine," Zara said, inhaling the delicious sage-infused steam rising from her bowl.

"It's not the same with the bought stuff," I replied. "Okay, enough about gnocchi." I poured wine into glasses. "I have something else to talk to you guys about." I looked around the table at my closest friends in the world. "It all started when I met Ryan Davenport on my birthday."

"Well there's a name we haven't heard much of lately. Have you spoken to him? Is he back from London?" Audrey asked excitedly.

"Let me get this out, Aud," I said.

"Sorry. Go on."

"You all know I've been seeing a grief counsellor for the past few months."

Zara and Audrey both nodded.

"So what sage advice did she have?" Jason asked, waving a piece of gnocchi on his fork. A note of cynicism was evident in his tone.

"She listened, mostly. You see, for ten years, I've been convinced I had everything under control. I thought if I shut myself off, I could avoid more suffering."

"And Ryan changed that?" Zara asked.

I couldn't help smiling thinking back to the moment I first saw him by my table in the café. "Yes. Ryan made me feel something I'd never felt before. Something… life changing." I held my hand over my heart. "For the first time, I felt out of control – and I liked it. Unfortunately, I was still a confused and fucked-up mess, and he had his own set of issues, too. Together, we were a disaster." I looked at my three closest friends who had been so incredibly supportive over the years. "I'm really sorry for dragging you guys along for the ride."

"We're just glad you're confronting all of this now," Audrey said, smiling.

"I've wanted to tell you what's been going on, but I wanted to wait until I'd gotten my thoughts straight."

"It's fine, Hol," Zara said. "We could tell you were okay, or we would have kicked your butt some more. At least, I would have."

"Well, I have the three of you to thank for it. Zara, I did need that kick up the butt. Jason, I know I bit your head off when you told me I hadn't dealt with my mother's death – it hit a nerve, probably because I knew it was true."

Jason smiled and took a big mouthful of gnocchi.

"And Audrey," I looked to my very best friend. "Asking me to talk to my dad back in September was your greatest gift to me." I could see her eyes misting, which immediately made mine blur.

"I *also* lost your mum that day, remember. I miss her, too. But I also miss the old Holly." A few tears slipped down her cheeks. "I can see that person coming back."

"Jesus Christ," Jason said, exhaling loudly.

"Okay, okay," I stated firmly, smiling. "That's the emotional part of the evening over. I'm sorry to be a downer on Christmas Eve. Now, can you lot please eat? I slaved over this."

"That's the complete opposite of a downer. You and Ryan are going to live happily ever after and have lots of super-gorgeous babies," Audrey said, wiping her eyes with her napkin.

"Oh, God. Steady on. Don't go marrying me off just yet!"

"Hmmm, mmmm." Audrey tried unsuccessfully to respond around a mouthful of gnocchi.

"So, Ryan is still it for you?" Jason asked, a look of calm resignation on his face.

"I'm in love with him." I said it out loud and I knew it was true. "He's my same-page person."

Audrey and Zara beamed. Even Jason smiled. Our foursome was intact. I just needed to win back my man.

"So what's the plan? Are you going to fly to London?" Zara asked.

"Ooh yes! A grand, romantic gesture!" Audrey exclaimed.

"Turns out I won't have to. You know how I've been catching up with Ryan's mum?"

They all nodded, their mouths full.

"Well, she's invited me to her engagement party on New Year's Eve. Ryan's flying into Sydney on Boxing Day, so I'm going to surprise him at the airport. That's my grand plan."

"Holy shit!" Zara chimed in. "That's really romantic."

We finished our meals, along with several bottles of wine. I felt a fire burning inside me – I knew this was the right path. From that point on, I was determined to be honest, brave and open with the people I loved.

***

I spent Christmas Day with my family at Dad's new apartment at Balmoral Beach. Sophie, Dad's girlfriend, also joined us. She was the one who had suggested that Dad see a counsellor. Soon after selling the house, he had asked her out to lunch, and things progressed from there. Sophie really seemed to make him happy, and I found it surprisingly painless seeing him with another woman. He deserved a second chance at love.

After lunch, we sat around the table on the balcony admiring the serene beauty of the unique harbour view.

"I could sleep for a week I'm so full," April said, yawning.

"Me too," I agreed.

"It might be the turkey you ate for lunch," Jamie suggested. "It's soporific."

"What the hell does 'soporific' mean?" April asked.

"A drug or other substance that induces drowsiness or sleep," Jamie replied matter of factly.

"What are you?" April laughed. "A walking dictionary?"

"I did an assignment on sleep therapies this year. I think I might like to be some kind of sleep analyst when I finish school."

"Is that someone's phone ringing?" Dad asked suddenly.

"Oh yes, that's me. Sorry, Jamie. I want to know more about this sleep stuff and what turkeys have to do with it. Sounds like gobbledegook to me. Get it? Turkey... Gobble?" I laughed to myself as I went inside to answer my phone. I didn't look at the number before answering.

"Merry Christmas, Holly speaking." I was still laughing at my silly turkey joke.

"Well, Merry Christmas to you, too, Holly."

Ryan.

"Oh ... um ... hi..." *Silence*

Suddenly, I was wide awake. Shouldn't he be on a plane? Perhaps he was at Singapore airport.

"I hope I haven't interrupted your Christmas lunch."

I closed my eyes as he spoke, enjoying the sound of his voice.

"Oh, no. We've finished. We were just sitting outside enjoying the view."

"I just wanted to wish you a merry Christmas."

"Thank you. You too. How are you?"

"I'm good. Dad's been here for a few weeks."

"Oh, okay. How is your dad?"

I was hoping he would tell me himself about his dad's reaction to the divorce and the upcoming engagement party.

"Dad's fine." He paused before continuing. "He just needed a holiday."

"Fair enough."

Pause

"Anyway, Holly, I just wanted to wish you a merry Christmas."

"You already did."

"Oh." *Pause.* "Sorry." *Pause.* "Take care of yourself, Holly." *Silence.*

He ended the call before I could say goodbye. I stared at my phone for several seconds. *What the hell was that?*

He hadn't even mentioned his mother's engagement party or that he would be in Sydney in less than twenty-four hours. Jessica would have told me if there had been a change of plans. I was more determined than ever to see him at the airport and find out where his head was at. It had been months since we'd last spoken. I needed to see him face-to-face. Unless something had changed for him, our unparalleled physical attraction would be hard to ignore. I was in a far better place than when we were last together. He was the only unknown quantity. But the fact that he called must mean he still thought of me.

When I returned to the balcony, April was dozing on one of the sun lounges. Jamie was still talking animatedly about her interest in sleep therapy. I spent the rest of the day enjoying the sunshine and the company of my beautiful family.

Chapter Twenty-Nine

Ryan's flight was due in at six on Monday morning, so he probably wouldn't be coming through the gate before seven. His mum had given me the details and had promised to keep my surprise a secret. I got there early. Airports are one of my favourite places – they offer the ultimate people-watching opportunities. Everyone is coming or going, and my "imagine-their-life" game can be ramped up to include exotic and faraway places.

The arrivals lounge at an international airport is a place of high emotion, excitement and anticipation. Young children with their mums awaiting the return of their father after a long business trip. Grandparents waiting to see the grandchildren they only see once a year, if they're lucky. Boyfriends waiting for their adventurous girlfriends to return from a girls' trip to Bali, hoping their relationship is still on track – or that she'd at least be on the flight.

Despite my best efforts to remain focused, I couldn't help imagining what would happen when Ryan walked through those gates. My imagination went a little overboard. I imagined him emerging, a little weary looking, pulling his suitcase behind him.

Still the best-looking man I'd seen by far, the hundreds of other passengers would fade away as soon as he appeared. His dark blonde hair would be a bit mussed up from the long-haul flight. As he got closer, our eyes would meet and he'd stop, completely shocked. For a painful couple of minutes, which would most likely only be seconds, we would stare at each other. Then he'd smile. Closing my eyes, I sucked in a breath as the memory of his smile simultaneously allowed me to breathe again and left me breathless.

"Hi," he'd mouth, without closing the distance.

I'd duck under the barrier and rush forward. When I reached him, he'd sweep me off my feet and kiss me with an urgency I knew had always been right there simmering below the surface, just waiting for the green light. My legs would instinctively wrap around his waist and I would kiss him back, matching his desperation heartbeat for heartbeat.

Shaking my head to clear the daydream that I hoped was about to become a reality, I glanced up at the arrivals gate. He had already passed through and was halfway down the walkway. He had stopped in his tracks. Our eyes locked, and for a second, time stood still.

Then time went from standing still to racing at a hundred miles an hour. My vision expanded to the woman standing next to him. Her confused gaze alternated between Ryan and me.

He wasn't travelling alone.

Maybe she's just a work colleague.

Maybe not.

Wanting to run, I felt betrayed by my jelly legs. Slowly, Ryan and the woman – who I already despised for no solid reason – walked towards me. My brain was screaming at my legs to sort themselves out in case they were needed. Again, no joy. It felt like my feet were bolted to the floor. If I'd tried to move, I would have fallen flat on my face.

"Hello," said the woman. "Are you our ride?"

Is she fucking serious? Her pompous English accent and condescending tone snapped me out of my stupor.

"Err… No. Why would you think that?" I replied in a far more cutting tone than necessary.

"Christ. Holly. Sorry," Ryan interrupted. "What are you doing here?"

Think, Holly. For God's sake. Think!

"Hello, Ryan." I managed to sound borderline calm. "What a coincidence. I'm here to meet Audrey. She's flying in from… um… from…" *Shit, think of one goddamn place in the world. Anywhere!* "Adelaide."

Phew!

"Oh really?" Ryan appeared puzzled. "Why are you at the international terminal?"

Shit.

"Oh. Right. I'm at the wrong place." This was so freaking embarrassing. "I'd better run. Good to see you again, Ryan, and… sorry, I didn't catch your name." I tried to smile when I looked at the woman.

"Oh, sorry." Ryan looked at the woman, then back at me awkwardly. "Holly, this is Rachael. She works for Preston Finance. She's here to view the progress of the Aqua Vue project."

Okay, good. Work colleague.

"And for your mother's engagement party." Her smug tone made me want to punch her.

Maybe not.

"This is Holly Ashton," Ryan continued. "She's my architect for the project."

She raised her eyebrows. "Oh wow. It really is a coincidence to see you here." She didn't believe it was a coincidence for a second. "Come on, babe. Can we get going?"

Babe? That one little word spoke volumes about their status. I felt like my heart was being ripped out.

"Nice to meet you, Rachael." I shook hands with her. "I'd better go. Audrey will be wondering where I am." My lie was even more embarrassing now.

I didn't look at Ryan. I just turned on my heel and walked away, trying not to break into a flat-out run.

Chapter Thirty

"Thanks for meeting me, Holly."

It had been five days since my mortifying airport experience. Ryan had called my phone a number of times. I ignored them all.

Jessica Davenport had called me yesterday asking if I'd meet her for a coffee in the botanical gardens café. She and I had forged an unlikely friendship over the last few months. I'd even been out to dinner with her and Jonathan a few times. She reminded me of my own mother. My friendship with her was how I imagined my relationship with my mum would have been. Jessica had called me the day Ryan had arrived with Rachael to see if I was okay. Like me, she had been blindsided by Rachael's presence.

"Does Ryan know you're here with me?" I asked.

"No. I've only seen him once since he arrived. He came over for dinner two nights ago and was clearly miserable. He was smart enough not to bring Rachael. She's a gold-digging bitch. Always was."

"What do you mean, 'always was'?"

"Rachael and Ryan dated for about a year in London. I met her a couple of times when I was over there visiting. I disliked her immensely."

I freaking loved this woman!

"Oh! He mentioned a long-term relationship. He told me she wanted to take it to the next level, but it never felt right, so he broke it off."

His words, which had meant so much to me at the time, came flooding back.

And now I know why nothing ever felt right. They weren't you.

"He's hurting, Holly. It's my fault, and Daniel's, for being such horrible role models for him growing up. We were always arguing." She was silent for a few moments. "It's no wonder he's so against commitment."

"Maybe Rachael is good for him. Maybe she's what he needs right now." I didn't want to believe that, but he was with her. Not me.

"Look, I've found the love of my life now in Jonathan. I don't want Ryan making the same mistakes I did. I'm begging you, please come to the party tomorrow night."

"I can't come to your engagement party, Jessica," I stated firmly. "I'm really happy for you. I am. But I can't face seeing him with Ra… with her."

"You need to look at this from another angle."

Now she was speaking my language. Actually, she was speaking my mother's language. *Shit.*

"What do you mean?" I asked tentatively.

"It's New Year's Eve tomorrow. We chose the date for our engagement party for a reason. It's the end and the beginning in one night. I'm going to say goodbye to my first marriage and welcome in my new one. I'm starting afresh."

Tears welled in my eyes. I couldn't speak.

"You need to come to the party. You need to say goodbye to this year. It's been life-changing for you in so many ways." She reached across the table and held my hands. "I'm not your mother, Holly. But I care about you. I want you to welcome in the new year, with or without my son. I'm hopeful it will be with him, but if not, get some closure so you can move on with an open heart."

"I'm not sure I'm ready for that, Jessica."

"Please think about it. I'd really like you to be there."

"Okay," I conceded. "I'll think about it."

"Great!" She waved the waiter over for the bill. "Now let's go and find you something incredible to wear. At the very least, you can knock him sideways." She laughed, and I couldn't help laughing, too.

We spent hours at the shops. Jessica made me try on about a thousand dresses – she was even worse than Audrey. I loved every second of it.

"This is the one!" she exclaimed when I came out of the dressing room in a gorgeous red dress. "You are going to outshine every female on the island."

"Oh God, I hope not!" I exclaimed. "No one should outshine the bride-to-be."

"Oh please. I'm too old to be a bridezilla."

Jessica looked absolutely incredible. She was tall and slim. Her dark blonde hair appeared to have silver highlights rather than being grey. Her olive skin, whilst showing the inevitable signs of ageing, glowed. She was the poster girl for ageing gracefully.

"I do really love this dress." I smoothed my hands down the fitted gown. It had my favourite asymmetrical neckline. It hugged my body all the way to the floor, with a slit up the side – sexy with a little mystery. Even I could admit the dress was made for me.

"Well, that's settled then. This is the dress you'll wear. Rachael will disappear into the background, and Ryan won't stand a chance."

"I still haven't decided whether I'm even coming."

"You'll be there."

Chapter Thirty-One

"Why aren't you dressed?" Audrey asked. "It's New Year's Eve, and you've got a party to go to. Hurry up or you'll miss the boat."

"I'm not sure I can go," I replied, not taking my eyes off the television coverage of the Sydney Harbour festivities.

"Of course you're going." She grabbed my arm and pulled me up. "You have to see him, Holly. Otherwise you'll just mope for the rest of the holidays."

"I'm happy here on the couch." I knew I was being a chicken, but the truth was, I was terrified of seeing him with her again.

"Well, if you're not going to Jessica's engagement party, you at least have to come with us to Moon. Corey and his mates are coming. Jake is DJing. He gave Zara a bunch of spare tickets."

"I don't know, Aud. I feel bad for not going to the party, but I think I've hesitated too long."

"For God's sake, girl." She clapped her hands and waved me towards my bedroom. "Get up, grab a quick shower and throw on that killer dress. I'll help you with your hair and makeup."

"Okay, okay, I'm going!" Jumping up, I raced for the shower. Audrey's nudge was exactly what I'd needed.

Jessica had become important to me, and I was genuinely happy for her and Jonathan. I wanted to be there for them. If I'd learnt anything this year, it was that I was strong. Much stronger than I gave myself credit for. Of course, I was devastated that Ryan had moved on. However, I was rebuilding my life, and part of that was being honest and being brave. Tonight, I would have to be brave.

Looking in the full-length mirror, I took confidence from the beautiful dress hugging my body. I felt confident in it. Audrey advised me to leave my hair out, so I just swept it over my shoulder. She worked her magic on my face, somehow highlighting my eyes without it looking like I had makeup on at all. Black, strappy heels completed my outfit. Well, almost. I reached for my charm bracelet and carefully attached the clasp around my wrist. I couldn't help holding the tiny hummingbird between my fingers. Despite the fact that Ryan had moved on, it was a tiny reminder of our connection, and I would never take it off.

"If you've missed the boat, you can take a water taxi from East Circular Quay. They'll take you directly to Fort Denison."

"Okay, thanks, Aud." I looked her in the eyes. "Tell me I can do this."

"Of course you can do it, Hol." She hugged me, then pulled back. "You *need* to do this. Show him the confident, strong and caring woman you've found these past few months." She looked at my reflection in the mirror. "Show him what he's missing."

"Okay, I'll go – for Jessica and Jonathan. If Ryan wants to talk, I'll have my game face on." I winked at her reflection.

"If it all goes pear shaped, call me. I'll leave a ticket at the door at Moon."

"Deal."

Audrey drove me down to the quay. Getting a cab on New Year's Eve would be impossible, and I couldn't walk that far in heels. I settled into a seat in the water taxi and took in my surroundings. There were thousands of people lining the shore, all jostling for the best vantage point. It was just after eight o'clock, so the first round of fireworks would kick off in under an hour. The atmosphere was electric.

Fort Denison fascinated me. Originally, it was just a small, rocky island in Sydney Harbour. It was used to isolate convicts back in 1788. Then in the mid-1800s, the island was flattened and a defence fort was built. Now it's a restaurant and function centre.

As the water taxi drew closer, I could see a crowd of people milling around on Battery Lawn in front of the restaurant. My nerves kicked up a notch.

Breathe in, breathe out.

When we docked, the driver helped me out onto the small jetty. I deserved a medal for this level of bravery. Arriving solo to an engagement party for the mother of my ex-fling? Ex-boyfriend? Ex-God-knows-what? *What the hell am I doing here?*

Panicking, I turned back to my water taxi, but it had disappeared. I was stranded.

Right, Holly. Shoulders back, hold your head high. Go forth and be fabulous!

The sandstone steps led up to the lawn, where partygoers were sipping cocktails. I was sure I could blend into the crowd while I searched for Jessica. When I reached the top of the stairs, a waiter offered me a cocktail. I took it gratefully. I was going to need more than one.

The other guests were preoccupied with their own conversations, so I was fairly sure I could slip through the crowd unnoticed. Spotting Jessica at the other end of the lawn, I took a deep breath and started to make my way over.

"Why are you in such a hurry?"

A hand on my arm stopped my progress, and I looked up to see who the culprit was. I was relieved to see Toby, one of Ryan's mates.

"Oh hey, Toby. How are you?"

"I'm good." He looked me up and down and smiled. "You look fucking incredible. Does Ryan know you're here?"

"Err… thanks. And no. He doesn't know I'm coming." I stared at my shoes, feeling the heels sinking into the grass. "I'm here for Jessica and Jonathan."

"Right, sorry. I heard you guys split. He's a fucking idiot. Rachael's a drag."

"Yes, well. It's his life." I feigned being fine with it.

"Can I get you another drink?"

I'd catch Jessica later. "Sure, why not? Thanks."

Toby waved over one of the roving waiters, who promptly delivered another cocktail.

"Happy New Year, Holly," he said, raising his glass to mine.

"Happy New Year, Toby."

"Will you excuse me for a second? I've just seen Aspen, and I need to speak to her." He stepped forward and gave me a kiss on the cheek.

Before I had a chance to respond, Toby was wrenched backwards. Shocked, I wobbled backwards on my heels. I somehow managed to pull them out of the grass before I fell over.

Ryan.

"What the fuck?" Toby shouted.

Ryan didn't say anything in response. He was staring straight at me and appeared dumbstruck.

Toby shook his head, then disappeared into the crowd.

"What are you doing here, Holly?"

I couldn't help but laugh. "That seems to be all you have to say to me these days." I stopped laughing and looked directly into his tortured, sapphire eyes. "Don't worry. I'm not here for you. I'm here for your mother."

"What do you mean? You don't even know my mother. You met her once – the day we walked in on her having an affair!" Suddenly the party went quiet.

Jonathan appeared behind Ryan, closely followed by Jessica.

I had hoped to slip into the party. Instead, I was causing a scene.

"Darling," Jessica said, pushing past Jonathan. "Holly and I have become friends. I invited her tonight." She turned to me and gave me a hug. "Thank you so much for coming. You look amazing."

"So do you." She was wearing an emerald green cocktail dress that perfectly suited her figure and complexion. She looked beautiful. "Congratulations." I glanced at Jonathan, then back to her. "I'm sorry for causing a scene."

"Sorry, what the hell is going on here?" Ryan glared at Jessica as if she'd committed some sort of heinous crime. "How dare you invite her without telling me."

I felt about two inches tall. He was seriously pissed off that I was there. Perhaps he was worried it would upset his girlfriend.

Seething, I turned and started walking towards the restaurant. I needed to get away from him.

"Where are you going?" Ryan asked, sounding more upset than angry.

I didn't turn around. "Away from you."

I located the ladies' restroom and quickly entered, grateful for the relative sanctuary. I plonked my clutch on the vanity and stared at my reflection, shaking my head. I'd known it would be a mistake to come here. I briefly considered calling a water taxi to retrieve me but decided to soldier on. Touching up my lip gloss, I smiled to myself. Ryan wasn't going to take away my confidence. He had no right.

Opening the door to the bathroom, I walked directly into a warm, firm chest. Looking up, sapphire eyes ripped through my steely resolve, and I was momentarily mesmerised.

Ryan didn't speak. He just took my hand and led me down the corridor and then out a door on the opposite side of the restaurant. We emerged in a private area at the western end of the island, looking directly back at the bridge.

"Why did you bring me out here?" I asked, barely able to look him in the eye.

Before I knew what was happening, I was enveloped in his embrace. He held me as if I was the most precious thing in the world, and for a few moments, I just enjoyed being close to him again. I pulled out of his arms, and his hands immediately cupped my face.

"You look…" His eyes took in my body while his hands still held my face. "You look drop-dead fucking gorgeous, Holly."

"Thank you," I croaked.

"Why didn't you tell me you were coming tonight? I've tried calling you every day since I flew in." His hands went into his pockets. I took a quick moment to appreciate Ryan Davenport in a tuxedo. He had never looked so handsome. I wanted to throw my arms around his neck and kiss him senseless. The attraction between us was alive and well. If anything, it had never been stronger.

"I didn't know what to say. I didn't know how you'd react to my friendship with your mother. And seeing you at the airport with *her*..." It was as if her name were poison. I just couldn't say it out loud. "I just didn't think we had anything to talk about."

A loud bang scared the living daylights out of me. Ryan didn't flinch. He kept his gaze on me. His back was to the Harbour Bridge, and he was suddenly backlit by fireworks exploding everywhere. Rockets shot off from the bridge, and the sky became a smoky mass of colour and light. The display was choreographed to match the music blaring from all the boats bobbing on the harbour. Ryan stepped forward and again cupped my face. My heart raced and my breathing slowed. I thought I might pass out.

He leaned in so close I could feel his laboured breath on my lips. He was going to kiss me. *No, no, no!*

Pushing him back, I shook my head. "Rachael will be wondering where you are." *There, I said her name.*

"I don't give a shit about Rachael."

"Really? That's good to know, Ryan," Rachael said, appearing seemingly out of nowhere.

"Can you excuse us, Holly?" Rachael asked in an icy tone. "I think you might be in the wrong place again." *Sarcastic bitch.*

"Sure. I was just leaving anyway."

"To be honest, I have no idea why you'd be here in the first place."

"That's enough, Rachael," Ryan said sternly.

Her attempts to patronise me were not going to work. I had every right to be there.

"Jessica invited me." Giving her my trademark ice-queen glare, I stalked off. If that was who he'd replaced me with, good luck to him.

"Fucking hell." Ryan's voice stopped me in my tracks. "Holly, wait."

I couldn't resist turning around. "What?"

"This isn't what it seems." His face was desolate; he appeared broken.

"You're with Rachael now, Ryan." I gave him a half-smile. "It's exactly as it seems."

Turning on my heel, I opened the door and returned to the party.

Jessica quickly found me.

"Are you okay, darling?"

"I'm fine." I wasn't, but I would be. "Sorry again for before. I hope it hasn't ruined your evening."

"Of course it hasn't." She grabbed my hand and squeezed it gently. "Come on, I'll introduce you around."

The next three hours flew by as I drank cocktails and chatted to some very interesting people. Aspen, Ryan's younger sister, was the highlight of the evening for me. She and I bonded immediately. The tension I had felt earlier eased a little. Ryan and I locked eyes on a number of occasions. I was always the one to break the contact. It was hard to look at him without feeling that familiar stab through the heart. Rachael flitted around the crowd as if they were all there for her. She reminded me so much of Eva McCormack. I really didn't need another Eva in my life.

Glancing at my watch, I realised it was fifteen minutes until midnight. The year was nearly over. Someone tapped a champagne glass, signalling it was time for a speech.

"Can I have everyone's attention, please?" Jessica's voice came over the sound system.

A small podium with a microphone had been set up on the lawn. She and Jonathan were standing on it, holding hands. I glanced over at Ryan and saw that he was once again staring back at me. Rachael appeared at his side. I turned back to focus on Jessica.

When everyone was relatively quiet, she continued. "Thank you, everyone, for joining us this evening to celebrate our engagement." The crowd erupted. She smiled while she waited for the noise to die down again. "New Year's Eve is traditionally a night for celebration, so there seemed no better night for us to have this party." She looked around and stopped when she found me. Her gaze remained on me while she continued to speak. "As this year comes to an end, I'm going to say farewell to my past. I haven't always made the best choices in my life. Fortunately, two of the most incredible people in this world were the result of one of those choices. For that, I will be forever grateful." Slightly teary, she held up her glass and looked at Ryan and Aspen, who were standing side by side. Aspen raised her glass. Ryan was ashen. Part of me wanted to go over and hold his hand.

"When midnight strikes in just a few minutes' time, I move

forward to the next chapter of my life with an open heart, full of love for the man standing here beside me." She turned and looked at her fiancé. "Jonathan, you are the love of my life. It took me forever to find you, but better late than never." He kissed her with such obvious adoration and love, I had to look away.

Dabbing my eyes with a tissue, I glanced over at Ryan, who was staring at his mother. He then looked at me with what appeared to be hope in his eyes.

Boom! Suddenly, there were fireworks everywhere. "Happy New Year!" Jessica and Jonathan shouted into the microphone.

I was taken by surprise as Aspen grabbed my hand and dragged me around to get more drinks. We were continually stopped by guests wanting to wish us a happy new year or claim a midnight kiss.

It was impossible for me to avoid subtly glancing around, looking for Ryan. Unfortunately, I spotted him at the exact moment he spotted me. He was kissing Rachael. Her back was to me. Ryan had opened his eyes at the exact moment I realised what I was seeing. Saving myself further heartache, I quickly looked away.

"What's up with you and my brother?" Aspen asked.

The midnight excitement had dulled down, and we were finally able to have a conversation without constant interruption.

"Nothing." I downed the rest of my champagne. "Absolutely nothing."

"Well, that's disappointing. I much prefer you to that Rachael snob." She hooked her arm through mine. "My brother's an idiot." She slurred her words a little.

"I've been hearing that a bit lately." I bumped my shoulder gently against hers. "How do we get off this bloody island?"

"There's a boat to take guests back to the quay." She looked at me with a horrified expression. "You're not going home, are you?"

All I wanted to do was curl up in bed. If I was going to start the new year afresh, I needed to get some sleep.

"I was thinking about it. My feet are killing me."

"Seriously, Holly. No way! My best friend, Gemma, just texted me. She and her boyfriend want to meet up."

"Well, my friends are at a club. We could go there for a while if you like?"

"Oh my God, yes! I'll text Gemma. Where is it?"

Realising my desire to hide from the world was the old me, I gave her the details, then texted Audrey to tell her we were on our way. I was going to start the year with my best friends. It was no longer about shielding my heart from heartbreak. It was about acceptance.

I didn't need a new plan. I needed a new angle. Ryan may not have been my forever. He did, however, give me something precious. He gave me back my ability to love with an open heart. Even his blatant rejection hadn't done the damage it would have six months ago. I was stronger. I was determined. I was Anna Wilson's daughter.

"Let's go." I grabbed Aspen's hand and pulled her along the lawn towards the boat jetty.

"Where are you two going?" Ryan's voice interrupted my focus.

Aspen looked up at her brother. I didn't.

"None of your business," she replied bluntly.

"Don't be a child, Aspen."

"I'm twenty-five years old, Ryan. Don't patronise me. Go find your snobby girlfriend and leave us alone. And by the way, are you out of your freaking mind?"

"Don't interfere, little sister. You don't know what you're talking about."

"Oh my God. Could you be any more condescending? I understand plenty." She waved her hands up and down towards me. "Here is a stunning, smart and caring girl who you ditched for a snobby cow who looks down on everyone and everything. What did I miss exactly?"

I couldn't resist sneaking a quick glance at Ryan. His expression was a confusing combination of anger and melancholy. I had the overwhelming urge to hug him. So I did. It must have been the cocktails.

My body melded to his as if it remembered every contour of his chest. His arms wrapped around me. He buried his face in the crook of my neck. His right hand came up and caressed the back of my head – both protective and possessive. It reminded me of the many nights we lay naked together in bed, so completely at peace. But now someone else shared his bed.

Aspen was noisily clearing her throat. Reluctantly, I pushed him away and looked into his sad eyes.

"We're going to meet my friends at a club." I gave him my best attempt at a smile. "I'll make sure Aspen gets home, otherwise she can stay at mine."

"We need to talk, Holly."

"I'm not sure we do." I broke eye contact, mainly because I

couldn't stand looking at his beautiful eyes, so full of pain. "You've made your choice, and I have to live with that."

"That's the problem." He tilted my chin up, forcing me to look at him. He leant forward and whispered in my ear. "I can't."

"The boat's here," Aspen interrupted. "Let's go clubbing!" She grabbed my hand and started pulling me away from Ryan.

Ryan wouldn't let my hand go, and suddenly I was being pulled in two different directions. I dug my heels in and yanked my hands away from both of them.

"Aspen, give me a second with Ryan, okay? I'll catch up."

"Don't be too long. It's too far to swim."

I smiled and nodded, then watched her walk away, leaving us alone.

"Thank you." Ryan reached for me again, but I held my hands up.

"Look. You obviously have a girlfriend. I'll admit I'm not happy about it. If I'm completely honest, I was devastated when I saw you with her at the airport. But it's shown me I was wrong about us." I braced myself with a few deep breaths. "I'm taking your mother's advice and starting the new year afresh. I need you to respect that and leave me alone."

"What do you mean you were wrong about us?"

"It doesn't matter now. You moved on." I shrugged, then glanced towards the steps. "I've got to go, Ryan. I'm going to miss the boat."

"I think I already have," he chuckled sadly.

Rachael appeared by his side and took his hand. She kissed his cheek, which made me want to throw up.

"Come on, darling. There's a private yacht for family." She

looked down at me as she stressed the word *family*.

"There you go, Ryan. You haven't missed the boat. You're just catching a different one." I took a step closer to him, glared at Rachel, then kissed Ryan gently on the cheek. "Happy New Year." Stepping back, I looked at him, then her, then back to him. I took another step back, then turned and walked towards the steps.

Ryan and I were not on the same page, the same chapter or even the same book anymore. He had found a new book. Well, a trashy magazine at least. Good luck to him.

One foot in front of the other. Breathe in, breathe out.

I didn't trip. I didn't stumble. I descended the steps gracefully and boarded the boat. I felt sapphire eyes burning into me. I didn't look back.

**

When Aspen and I got to Moon, Gemma was waiting for us out the front with her boyfriend, Tai.

"Where's Ryan?"

"Don't ask," Aspen replied.

"Come on, let's go in," I suggested. "There'll be tickets for us at the door."

The atmosphere at Moon was electric. The dance floor was crowded, and the music was thumping through the speakers. Jake really knew how to keep the party going. I spotted Audrey and Corey by the bar, so I signalled that we should head that way.

"Happy New Year!" I screamed, hugging Audrey and Corey from behind.

"Holly!" Audrey screamed back. "You made it."

"Audrey and Corey, this is Aspen, Ryan's sister, Gemma, and her boyfriend, Tai."

"Don't hold it against me," Aspen said, holding her hands up and laughing.

Audrey laughed but turned to me. "Didn't go so well with Ryan?"

"I'll tell you about it tomorrow. It's too noisy in here."

The music was thumping through my chest. It felt good.

"Where are Zara and Jase?" I asked, trying not to scream in her ear.

"I think they're on the dance floor."

Corey handed us a glass of bubbles each, then whispered in my ear. "Sam is here somewhere, too. I think he was hoping you would come."

"Thanks for the heads-up." I shook my head and took a big gulp of my drink.

"Come on. Let's dance," Gemma said. She grabbed Aspen by the hand, who in turn grabbed mine. Tai stayed at the bar with Corey and Audrey to finish his beer.

We lost ourselves in the throng of sweaty bodies. Before long, I was aware of hands on my hips and a body moving right up against my back.

"You're here."

I recognised Sam's voice in my ear. I didn't turn around.

Jason appeared at my side. "Are you okay?" he shouted into my ear.

I nodded rather than shouting back. Sam's arms wrapped around my waist and pulled me back. Although I didn't want

Sam the way I wanted Ryan, I couldn't deny I enjoyed the attention.

"Happy New Year, Holly." He kissed my cheek, then turned to acknowledge my new friends.

"Smile, Holly." Aspen took a photo of Sam and me with her phone. I looked back at Sam, blinded by the flash. Aspen laughed, then turned to Jason.

The music may have been deafening, but you'd have to have been blind to miss the instant attraction between them. Their eyes lit up, and the flirtation commenced immediately. I realised I had no idea about Aspen's relationship status, but I figured if there was a significant other, they would have been at the engagement party.

Sam turned me around to face him and drew me in so I was flush against him. Looking him in the eye, I realised this wasn't what I wanted. I no longer needed the emotional detachment of casual sex. Putting my hands on his chest, I pushed him away gently.

"Sorry, Sam. This isn't going to happen."

I turned and walked away to rejoin Audrey at the bar.

"Good on you," she said when I sat on the bar stool next to her.

"Thanks. I just want to have a drink with my best friend, then head home to bed." I waved to the bartender and ordered one more drink. "It's been a big night, and I'm exhausted."

"Well, I'm proud of you, Hol." She chinked her glass to mine. "This year is going to be a good one."

"Happy New Year, Audrey."

I finished my drink, then worked my way around the club to

say my goodbyes. Jason and Aspen were the hardest to find. They had retreated to a quieter corner of the club and were deep in conversation.

"I'm done, guys." I said, tapping Jason on the shoulder. "What do you want to do, Aspen?"

She looked to Jason.

"I'll look after her." He blushed a little, which was sweet. "I'll come out and see you into a cab." He turned to Aspen. "Can you give me five minutes?"

"Of course. I'll see what Gemma's up to." She gave me a big hug and squeezed me so tight I couldn't breathe. "I had a great time with you tonight, Holly. I'm so angry at my crazy brother."

"Don't be." I kissed her on the cheek and promised to keep in touch.

Chapter Thirty-Two

Safely in the cab, I pulled out my phone to see what time it was. I had three missed calls and two text messages from Ryan.

A little concerned, I called him back.

He answered on the first ring. "Are you with him?"

"What are you talking about?"

"Just tell me you're not with him."

"Who?"

"Aspen texted me photos of you looking very cosy with that Tresswells asshole. I'm going out of my mind here."

"Err… firstly, it's none of your damn business, and secondly, don't be such a bloody hypocrite. You're with your girlfriend. Remember?" I took a deep breath. "I told you at the party you need to leave me alone and let me move on. Apparently, you didn't have any problems moving on from me. Maybe you can give me some tips?"

"I'm really not in the mood for your smart mouth, Holly."

"Well that works out well then, doesn't it? It's three in the morning. I'm going home. Happy New Year, Ryan."

"Wait! She's not here. Rachael and I broke up."

Pause.

"Please, Holly. This is killing me. I need to see you."

Pause.

"Please come and I'll explain everything."

Long pause,

"Okay, fine, I'll come. But I won't stay long."

"Okay," he exhaled. "See you soon."

Despite my enraged brain telling me I was a gullible moron, my heart refused to listen. I heard myself asking the cab driver to head north across the bridge. I heard myself telling him Ryan's address. What I didn't hear was fear or regret in my voice. This man was fundamentally important to me. Whatever he had to say, I was going to listen. And then I was going to go home.

As I rode the lift up to the top floor, I stared at my reflection in the mirrored wall. I couldn't help smiling. If the eyes really are the window to your soul, I was more at peace than I'd been for ten years. More green than grey, Mum's eyes looked back at me. The vacant stare that had haunted me since I said goodbye to her in the hospital room was gone. It was one of the demons I had confronted and overcome. I could now remember her bright green eyes, expressing every emotion, every thought she'd ever had without the need for words. She talked with her eyes, and I had listened to every word they'd said.

The lift opened, and I walked with purpose to Ryan's door. It was slightly ajar. I pushed it open and entered his apartment. My heart was racing and those damn butterflies in my stomach were up to their usual antics, but it wasn't nerves I was feeling. That was just what happened whenever he was near.

Ryan stood with his back to me, staring out the floor-to-ceiling windows. I stopped before I reached him and cleared my throat.

Startled out of his thoughts, he turned around.

I was frozen to the spot, my heels pressing gently into the plush carpet of his luxurious lounge room.

Ryan's eyes moved down my body, then back up to meet my questioning eyes. I resisted the urge to cross my arms defensively over my chest. I wasn't there to hide; I was there to listen.

Locking his gaze to mine, he moved slowly towards me. He didn't speak; he didn't need to. His eyes expressed the love I knew he felt for me. I had no doubt he was seeing the same thing in mine. The whole world disappeared as he brought his lips to mine. His tongue sought entry, and I didn't deny him. As our kiss deepened, I felt my whole body sigh in relief.

"I missed you," he said, against my mouth.

"I missed you, too," I conceded. I had missed him so much, it hurt. But this wasn't what I had come here for.

"Wait." I pushed him away.

Ryan gave me a fierce look, as if he was about to go into battle.

"I just came here to talk. I'm not jumping straight into bed with you. A couple of hours ago, you had a girlfriend. A week ago, I hadn't heard from you in months."

Running his hands through his hair, he nodded. "I was hoping we could have sex now and talk later." He gave me a cheeky grin.

"Not how this works, buddy."

"Okay. Let's talk."

He took my hand and led me over to the lounge. We sat down.

"Did you really break up with Rachael? I saw you kissing her at midnight." The pain in my heart came back with the memory.

"She kissed me. I didn't kiss her back. She caught me by surprise – Holly, I pushed her away." He cupped my face. "I'm sorry you had to see that." He started feathering kisses along my jawline and down my neck.

I batted him away.

"I'm confused, Ryan. So much has changed since you left. I'm not the same person anymore."

"I'm not the same person either. So much has happened. I want to tell you everything, but I'm having trouble concentrating with you in that dress."

"I don't think you'll concentrate any better with me out of the dress, if that's what you're implying?"

"I think it's worth a try." He edged closer. With his lips a hair's breadth away from mine, he slowly started unzipping my dress.

My breath hitched when I felt his fingers on my back. His lips moved to my collarbone. I knew he was trying to distract me from my interrogation.

"You brought a girlfriend to your mother's engagement party." My brain refused to give up just yet.

Sighing, he stopped unzipping and sat back so he could look at me. "Preston Finance was sending her out here in January anyway, to assess the Aqua Vue progress. Dad was over visiting me in London. They really hit it off, and he told her about Mum's party. She applied to fly out earlier on annual leave." He kissed my already-exposed shoulder. "By that time, I knew I had made a huge mistake getting back together with her, but it was too late."

"So you were planning on breaking up with her anyway?"

"Holly, I should never have gone there again."

"Why did you?" I whispered. I hated even thinking about him with another woman, but this was important.

It was as if I'd dumped a bucket of ice water on him. He bent over, his elbows propped on his knees, and ran his hands through his hair. He didn't say anything for a few minutes. I assumed he was contemplating his response.

I sat quietly and waited.

Eventually, he sat back and turned towards me, propping his knee on the lounge. He was now looking directly at me.

I drew in a breath, a little taken aback by his intense gaze.

He took hold of my hands. "You told me there was no hope for us. I was completely gutted." He stared at our hands, entwined together. "Deep down, I knew it wasn't true and that we both just needed space to sort out our heads. But I was a bit of a mess, thanks to my crazy parents. Rachael was everywhere. I guess I just gave in to it." The sorrow in his eyes, now boring into mine, spoke to me before he even said the next words. "I'm really sorry, Holly. Can you forgive me?"

"I understand the need to escape from your own head. I did it for years. But this wasn't just someone random. It was your ex-girlfriend. You told me yourself she had wanted more from you. How can I trust that if we do try to make this work, you won't just jet off to London and back to her bed any time we have a bump in the road?"

"Two reasons. One, I love you, and if I can get you back now, I won't ever let anything come between us again."

My heart skipped a beat and my eyes blurred.

"And two?" I croaked.

"The time I spent with my father in London opened my eyes to a few things. He is a drunk and a fool. My mother deserves a medal for putting up with him as long as she did."

"I'm sorry, Ryan."

"Don't be. I'm going to get him the help he needs. I came to realise my strongest relationship role models were just poorly matched. I won't be making the same mistake they did." He looked me in the eyes. "You are my match, Holly."

I smiled through my tears.

"Seeing my mum with Jonathan confirmed what I already knew. When you find your soulmate, they become your future, regardless of your past."

"I love you, too."

The words came without hesitation and with the full strength of meaning behind them.

"About bloody time. I didn't think I'd ever…"

"Shh," I interrupted him. "Sex now. Talk later."

"Thank God." Ryan pounced on me, kissing me hard. His weight pushed me down onto the lounge. He pulled back from me, propping his hands on either side of my head. "I love you so much."

"Show me." I fisted his shirt in my hand and pulled his mouth back to mine. I was ready for him to just take me right there, but Ryan had other ideas. "Come on. I'm going to at least try to take this slow."

Pulling me up, he took my hand and led me to his bedroom. When we reached his bed, I turned so he could finish undoing the zipper on my dress. He kissed my shoulder gently as the beautiful red material pooled at my feet. I stepped out of it and turned around.

Ryan's eyes shamelessly drifted over my body. His hands cupped my breasts, only partially hidden by my sheer, strapless bra and matching underwear.

"You are far more beautiful than my mind could possibly remember. I wasn't doing you justice in my fantasies."

Reaching back, I unclasped my bra. I dropped it to the floor without taking my eyes from Ryan's increasingly lust-filled gaze. When I hooked my thumbs in my underwear and pushed them down to join the bra, he looked like he might explode. Judging from his tented trousers, that seemed like a definite risk. Completely naked, I placed my hands on my hips and smiled. "Your turn."

Ryan ripped his clothes off like a man possessed. He wasn't going to give me a show. When he reached for me, I dodged his hand and pushed him back onto the bed. This time, I was taking control.

Ryan laughed, scuttling back up the bed and reclining against the wall of pillows. "I think I'm going to like this new Holly."

"Oh, you have no idea, Mr Davenport." I climbed on to the bed. Without any unnecessary foreplay, I straddled him. Taking him by surprise, I sank onto his impressive erection.

"Holy shit!" Ryan sat up and grabbed hold of my hips. "You weren't kidding."

Grinding down on him, I leant forward and kissed him hard. Our tongues went to war as our bodies connected in every conceivable way.

Wanting to feel him deeper, I sat up and leant back, resting my hands on his muscly thighs. His eyes were closed tight as he pushed up into me. Sensing my stare, he opened his eyes and smiled.

"Sorry about not taking it slow." It came out a little breathless as my body surged towards the release it craved.

"You are perfect." His voice matched mine as he struggled to keep his eyes open. He leant forward and took each of my breasts in his mouth, giving them equal attention. My head fell back in pure ecstasy. I was going higher and higher on every thrust.

"Come with me."

His ragged voice pushed me over the edge. In those following moments, I saw the real fireworks display of the evening. Both our bodies shuddered, and we clung to each other. We were together. We were as together as we could possibly be, and nothing was going to tear us apart.

"I love you." We said it in unison.

We lay together in silence, me draped across his chest, for a long time. The months apart and the less-than-ideal road to our reunion had combined to mean the sex was beyond anything I'd experienced before.

Suddenly, I had a question, and I needed the answer immediately. I couldn't believe I hadn't thought to ask it before.

"How long is Rachael in Sydney for?" I propped myself up on my elbows.

"Talk about a buzzkill, Holly." He stroked my hair and cupped my chin. "I just had the most mind-blowing sex of my life. I'd like to enjoy it for a few more minutes, and then I'd like to get some sleep. It's nearly five in the morning. Can we talk about this later?"

Impatient by nature, I poked him in the ribs. "If you tell me now and I like the answer, I might be ready for a repeat performance soon."

"What if you don't like the answer?"

"Just tell me."

"Ugh." His arm went across his face. "She's here for a while. Preston Finance invests in a number of Australian projects. It's not just Aqua Vue that brought her out here."

"Great." I slumped back on his chest. Ryan kissed my head.

"No repeat performance, I'm assuming."

"I think we could both use some sleep, don't you?"

"I'm sorry, Holly. She won't cause any problems between us."

I lifted my head from his chest so I could look at him.

"We're a done deal, Holly. You're mine now."

"I still don't belong to you, Ryan."

He laughed. "I forgot how argumentative you can be. But okay, we're officially together. If you see that Tresswells guy again, make sure he's clear about that."

Kissing his chest, I couldn't help smiling as I drifted off to sleep, wrapped in his arms.

Chapter Thirty-Three

Two weeks into the new year and we were both back to work. We'd barely spent a night apart, alternating between his apartment and mine.

Despite missing Mum just as much as always, I was determined to embrace life and the love I felt for Ryan rather than living in the past and dreading the future.

"Holly." Slater's voice broke through my reverie.

"I'm sorry. I was deep in thought. Lots of ideas for the Melbourne Project," I lied.

"It's okay, Holly." Mr Slater was so happy with my work, he was treating me with a new level of respect. "Can you pop over to the Aqua Vue site? Ryan's assistant just called. He has a few questions about the layout of one of the apartments and would like a face-to-face on site."

Building work had started at the end of last year when the approvals came through. After a few weeks' break over Christmas and New Year, work had finally restarted, and I was eager to see the progress. I tried to hide my smile, knowing Ryan was probably just finding an excuse to spend more time together.

"Of course. I'll go now."

I loved site visits. Watching a design come to life was truly exciting. Watching my own design come to life was beyond all my expectations. I visited the site every chance I got.

I donned my hard hat before entering the building and looking around. Glaziers were due any day to fit the expansive double-glazed windows. They would insulate the apartments year-round, reducing the carbon footprint of each one. Currently, however, they were open to the elements.

Standing at the edge of the street-level apartment, I was greeted by a spectacular, uninterrupted view of Lavender Bay and surrounds. The eight apartments were set at graduating levels going down to the water. The street level was the top, so from here I could see work happening on all the sub-levels. Leaning forward carefully, I waved to Jack, the site foreman, who was working on the next level down. He acknowledged me with a wave and a warm smile. As I stepped back from the edge, I was startled by a female voice.

"Incredible, isn't it?"

I spun around.

"Rachael?"

"How are you, Holly?"

Something in her tone made me glance around to see if Jack or any of the builders were able to still see me.

"I didn't know you'd be here," I said tentatively.

"Of course you didn't."

"Why are you here?"

She took a few steps towards me, and I glanced at the open drop behind me.

"I thought it was about time we had a little chat about how you stole my man."

"Excuse me?"

"You heard me, you little bitch." She was now close enough to poke me in the chest. "Ryan is mine. He was mine before he met you, and he'll be mine long after you're gone."

I really didn't like the way she said *gone*. She had crazy eyes. There was clearly no point arguing with her.

"So what's your plan here, Rachael?" Instead of retreating, I took a step towards her. It caught her off guard.

"My plan?"

"Well, you lied to get me here. I'm assuming you have a plan."

"Of course I do."

"So let's hear it."

She held up her left hand and waved a diamond ring in front of me. I felt the colour drain from my face.

"Ryan and I are getting married. He proposed in London, and we plan to tie the knot when we return to the UK next month. We hope to start a family – if we haven't already." She winked, rubbing her flat stomach.

Nauseous and completely blindsided, I stumbled backwards. Ryan had lied to me, and I had fallen for him all over again. *Hook, line and sinker.*

"You're a liar." My voice sounded weak and unsure.

"Look, darling, you've been a bit of fun for him. But it's time you stopped distracting him from his responsibilities." She gave me a stronger push with her manicured fingers. "He belongs with me."

My high heel caught on the uneven surface, and I stumbled backwards, knowing the edge was too close. It was a good twelve foot drop to the apartment below. Just before I fell, I saw the horrified look of the foreman watching from below. That cliché about seeing your life flash before your eyes as you plummet to inevitable doom is a load of crap. I just saw red. Then black. Then nothing.

Chapter Thirty-Four

Pain, blood, sweat, tool belt, sirens. Those were the things my brain could process as I drifted in and out of consciousness. The sirens got louder. Closer. Nothing made any sense except those bloody sirens. They made perfect sense. I was in trouble. Blackness descended again.

When I came to, I was in the back of an ambulance. I knew it straight away. A paramedic was trying to get an oxygen mask over my mouth. I couldn't move my neck – some sort of brace was restricting my movement. And the pain. My left leg was killing me.

"What happened to me? Am I dead?" I asked.

"Don't worry. We're getting you to the hospital, Holly. You'll be fine."

"Audrey," I whispered. "Call Audrey."

"The site foreman has made some calls. Just try to relax now."

I lifted the oxygen mask off my mouth. "So I'm not dead?"

"Definitely not dead. You had a nasty fall. The foreman broke your fall, but you still took a fair knock to the head, and your leg is almost certainly broken. You need to lie still, though.

You'll be properly assessed at the hospital."

I stared at the ambulance roof. One minute I'd been staring out across the bay, waiting for Ryan to arrive. The next, I was being attacked. I closed my eyes as I remembered the flash of Rachael's engagement ring. How could Ryan have done this to me? I had believed he was in love with me, that Rachael was a mistake he had put in the past.

The pain in my leg was becoming more distant as I drifted off into a drug-induced sleep.

When I woke up, I could smell jasmine. The hospital room was light, bordering on cheery. *Plantation shutters are a decadent window dressing for a hospital,* I thought to myself. Copious vases exploded with an array of beautiful flowers, including a large mass of jasmine. I suspected Dad was responsible for that arrangement.

"Good morning, Holly." A friendly-looking nurse with grey hair and kind eyes stood at the end of the bed, holding a chart. "You've had a lot of people worried. Your boyfriend, Ryan, has barely left your side. He'll be devastated he wasn't here when you woke up. I think he's getting coffee."

"Can you make sure he isn't allowed back in here, please? I don't want to see him yet."

The nurse looked confused but nodded.

"How long have I been out?"

"You've drifted in and out for the last couple of days."

My leg was in a pretty intense-looking cast and was suspended by some sort of contraption.

"How would you describe your pain level between zero and ten, with zero being none at all and ten being unbearable?"

"Four, maybe a five?" My heart is way beyond a ten.

A handsome, middle-aged man entered the room wearing a white coat. A stethoscope hung around his neck.

"Hello, Holly. My name is Doctor Asprey. How are you feeling?"

"I'm a rock-solid four and a half, thanks." I held up my green button for self-administering pain drugs. "But soon I'll feel nothing at all."

He smiled and took the chart from the nurse.

"You're one very lucky girl. If your fall hadn't been broken by the foreman, this could be a very different conversation."

"I know. Jack saved my life. I'd really like to thank him."

"You'll be able to do that soon. I'd like you to stay in a few more days for observation. We've done a CT scan on your head and spine, and there are no fractures. You're a tough one. There's no swelling on your brain, just a nasty bump on your head that will go down soon. The haematomas will disappear in time, too. Your pain medication should take care of any headaches, and the nurses will take care of your post-traumatic stress evaluation."

"And my leg?"

"It was a compound fracture, so we were able to operate without your consent. Your femur broke the skin, exposing you to air, dirt and bacteria. We needed to set the bone and close you up to avoid septicaemia. You'll be in a cast for at least six weeks, then we'll reassess."

"Thanks, doctor."

"Do you feel strong enough to talk to the police?" asked the nurse. "They're keen to get your statement."

"Sure, I guess. Can I see my family and friends first, though?

But please, keep Ryan away. I'll talk to him in my own time."

"Okay. I don't think he'll take the news well, but it's your call."

She disappeared out the door, and I sank back into my comfortable pillows – another thing I didn't expect in a hospital. Breathing in the jasmine, I closed my eyes, realising how lucky I'd been. My number obviously wasn't up.

Audrey barrelled through the door first, closely followed by Zara, Jason, Dad, April and Jamie.

"Why won't you let Ryan in?" Audrey asked. "They had to physically restrain him out there."

"He and Rachael are engaged." Saying it out loud, the pain was indescribable. I took a deep breath before explaining what Rachael had told me.

"Oh my God." Audrey looked stunned, as did everyone else in the room. "Did you know it was Ryan who had you transferred to this private hospital?"

"No, I didn't." That explained the fancy room. "Not sure why he bothered."

I spent the next twenty minutes being interrogated, hugged and fussed over. Trying to convince them I was okay was no small feat.

"Has Rachael been arrested?" Zara asked.

"No idea. I'm seeing the police after you lot."

"Right. Then we'll get out of here," Dad said, herding everyone out. "We'll be back later, sweetheart." He kissed my cheek. "I'm so glad you're okay."

"Thanks, Dad."

Once they were gone, two police officers approached me.

"Hello, Holly," the policewoman said. "I'm Sergeant Piper and this is Constable Hanrahan." She took out a black notebook and pen from the inside pocket of her leather jacket. "We have Ms Rachael Woods in custody. The foreman on site witnessed the incident. We'd just like to take your statement."

There wasn't much to tell. I told them about our conversation and Rachael's threatening words. They seemed to ask the same questions over and over, but eventually they seemed satisfied.

"Thank you, Holly. We'll be in touch."

I was startled by a commotion outside my room. The police officers walked towards the door just as Ryan burst in.

"Holly. Oh my God. Holly." He looked shattered. Stubble covered his usually clean-shaven face. His general appearance was dishevelled.

Two men, who looked like security guards, were hot on his heels. "She doesn't want to see you." They seemed frantic. "You have to leave."

The police officers acted quickly, taking him by the arm.

Despite my heartbreak, seeing him so distraught was unsettling. After all we'd been through, I'd let him tell me himself about his engagement. I could probably do with the closure.

"It's okay," I called. "He can stay."

"Are you sure?" Constable Hanrahan asked. "We can stay if you need us."

"Thank you. I'll be fine. He won't be staying long."

Ryan looked relieved, yet confused and dejected.

When we were alone, he approached my bed. I held my hand up. "That's close enough."

He sat down on one of the seats and ran his hands through his messy hair. Then he looked at me with bleary eyes.

"What's going on, Holly? Why wouldn't you let me see you? I've been losing my mind ever since I heard about your accident."

"It wasn't an accident, Ryan." I stared at the ceiling. I couldn't look at him. "Your fiancée pushed me."

Ryan pulled his chair closer and reached for my hand. I pulled it away so he couldn't touch me.

"What? What fiancée? What are you talking about?"

"Rachael has been arrested. She pushed me off the ledge."

"Holy shit, Holly. I'm so sorry. Thank God you're okay."

"Yes, well, I survived. You can go now. You have a wedding to arrange." I couldn't keep the sarcasm out of my words.

"What has that psycho said to you? She isn't my fiancée. There is no way I would marry her."

"Words, Ryan. They're just words. I saw her ring. She told me she might already be pregnant with your baby."

"Jesus Christ." He stood up and paced the room, his fingers laced behind his neck. He turned suddenly. "And you believed her? You didn't even think to ask me if it was true?"

"Oh, I'm sorry. I was busy being pushed off a ledge."

Ryan slumped back down in his seat and put his face in his hands.

I lay back on my pillows and stared at the ceiling. Niggling doubts were starting to seep into my consciousness.

Eventually, he stood up again, closed the distance between us and gently picked up my left hand.

"There's only one woman for me, Holly, and I'm looking at her."

The intensity of his words annihilated me.

"When I buy an engagement ring," he continued. "I can assure you I won't be putting it on anyone's finger but yours." He gently lifted my hand to his mouth and kissed it reverently.

I was the world's worst girlfriend. What was wrong with me? Was it my lack of relationship experience?

"I'm sorry, babe." Tears blocked my vision. "She was so convincing and I just… I just…" The lump in my throat was making it hard to speak. "I… I believed her. It made sense."

Ryan kissed me on the lips, caressing my head gently with his hand. "How could that possibly make sense? Crazy girl."

"I don't know. I guess I should have waited for you to confirm or deny."

"I wish you had just known it couldn't be true, but I guess we're not there yet, are we?"

I pulled him down so I could kiss him again. The relief I felt at having him so close was overwhelming. Thinking I'd lost him again had been so horrifying, and yet I could have resolved it so quickly. Clearly, I had more to work on with my counsellor.

"I spent over ten years convincing myself I didn't have a future."

Ryan sat back down but didn't let go of my hand.

"Relationships weren't something I ever entertained, for fear of anyone else going through what we went through when Mum died. I guess when I saw Rachael, I just reverted back to the old me, the one who always expected doom and gloom."

"I get it. I do. But we're in this together now, you and me. Remember, until recently, I never thought I'd want to fully commit to a woman. My parents had pretty much seen to that.

You changed all that for me. You are my future, and I want to be yours."

The pain in my heart had subsided, but the pain in my leg was becoming unbearable. I reached for the green button and gave it a few hard presses. Ryan's concerned look was endearing.

"Do you need a nurse? What can I do?"

"I'm okay. The drugs will kick in soon. I'm getting a bit tired, though. It's been a big day." The afternoon sun was streaming through the windows, filling the room with light. I couldn't help remembering the tiny, windowless room my mother had been in when she died.

"I'll let you get some sleep then, beautiful." He stood up and kissed me gently.

I grabbed his shirt and pulled him back down, demanding a better kiss. He obliged.

"I'm sorry I doubted you, Ryan," I whispered against his mouth.

"It's okay," he replied. "You can make it up to me when you're all fixed up." His chuckle was infectious.

"I look forward to that." I kissed him again quickly.

He walked towards the door, then glanced back. "I'll be back a bit later, okay?"

"I love you."

Striding with purpose back to my bedside, he cupped my face. "I love you too, Holly Rose Ashton. Don't you ever forget it."

Chapter Thirty-Five

"Are we going by boat?" I asked, smiling broadly.

"Of sorts. Hope you're not afraid of heights?" He winked and I laughed.

"I'm pretty sure heights aren't an issue at sea level." Squeezing his hand, I felt the warmth resonating through my body, knowing we were going back to the place it all started.

"I remember that day so clearly," he said, taking his hand from mine, then wrapping his arm around my shoulders.

Being late July, the cold winter winds were biting. Nestling into his side, we walked the short distance along the jetty to where Gary was waiting with his seaplane.

"Feels like another lifetime." I glanced down at my charm bracelet, where the tiny hummingbird swung alongside the oyster.

"How's the leg? You know I'm more than willing to carry you."

"My leg is fine, but thanks for the offer." I nudged him, and he pulled me in closer. "I'm really looking forward to going back to the Hummingbird."

He kissed my head. "Me too."

Gary helped us into the seaplane, and before we knew it, we were airborne. I was still blown away by the beauty of the city seen from above, but I think I might have squealed less than I did the first time. I was content to enjoy the fact that almost a whole year had passed since we last took this journey, and we were still together.

The difference this time was that we were officially together, madly in love and deliriously happy.

Six months had passed since the horrible incident at the building site. Thanks to a gun defence lawyer, Rachael avoided a criminal record – it couldn't be proven that she meant for me to fall. I refused to spend any time worrying about whether justice had been served. It was of no consequence to me. She was back in London, out of the picture and I had the man.

The cast came off my leg in early March, six weeks after leaving the hospital. The bone had healed well, and after a few months of hydrotherapy, I now felt completely back to normal.

Ryan had been my rock. At times, his overprotectiveness had irritated me. For several weeks after the cast was removed, he wouldn't let me carry my things or help out around the apartment – *our* apartment. When I first left the hospital, he had insisted I move in with him so he could take care of me. I never moved out. We were going to spend every night together anyway, so it made sense. I was sad to leave Audrey and Zara, but they were happy for me, and we saw each other all the time anyway.

When the Aqua Vue project was completed, Ryan sold all the apartments, abandoning his plan to keep one for himself. The incident with Rachael had tarnished the building for him, and there was no way in hell I was going to live there. I still suffered nightmares. At first, I would wake up in a cold sweat almost nightly. Ryan would sit bolt upright, as if he had been waiting. He would talk to me until I was relaxed enough to fall asleep again. He loved me with everything he had, and for the first time in my life, I felt I had everything to give in return.

The seaplane landing on the choppy waters snapped me back to the present.

"What were you thinking about?" Ryan asked, as we motored towards the Hummingbird jetty.

"I was just thinking about the last six months. Well, the last year really. A lot has happened since the last time we were here."

He leaned over and kissed me. "Some good, some bad and some just plain ugly. But we're here now, and we face it all together from here on in. Deal?"

"Deal." I kissed him again, then let Gary help me down.

Gemma came rushing over and hugged us both. "Welcome back. I've missed you guys."

"Hey, Gem," I said, giving her a kiss on the cheek. "How are you?"

"I'm great." She grabbed my hand and dragged me down the jetty. I glanced back at Ryan, picking up our bags. He smiled at me.

I did a double take as the private beach came into view. I could have sworn I recognised a few people. Looking more closely, I was shocked to see Audrey, Zara, Jason and Aspen. They held up a banner.

"Happy birthday, Holly!"

"Oh my God!" I exclaimed, holding my hands over my mouth.

I turned back to see Ryan's reaction. He was right behind me, looking smug.

"You planned this, didn't you?" I poked him in the chest, laughing.

I stopped laughing when Ryan dropped down on one knee, a small, blue Tiffany & Co. box in the palm of his hand. My hands went back to my mouth as my brain went into shock. Ryan gently took hold of them.

"Holly," he choked out, then cleared his throat. "This has been a big year for both of us in many ways. The most important moment of my life came exactly one year ago when I saw this stunningly gorgeous woman in a café, staring out the window. I knew immediately there was something special about her. It was love at first sight for me. We've had our ups and downs, but for me, you're it. You are the love of my life. You are my everything."

Tears flowed freely down my cheeks. I was nodding like a crazy person.

"I have to ask you first," Ryan laughed.

"Sorry," I choked.

"Holly. Will you do me the honour of becoming my wife?"

I nodded again, smiling like a Cheshire cat. "I will. Of course I will. I love you so much."

Ryan stood up and managed to slip the ring on my finger before I leapt into his arms. "I love you, too. Obviously."

With the sound of squealing and clapping in the background, we kissed. I wanted to stay like that forever. Enveloped in his arms, warmth spread throughout my body. He was my forever. He was my same-page person.

Chapter Thirty-Six

Ryan had arranged for everyone to stay overnight, as copious amounts of champagne and seaplanes would be a very unpleasant combination, I imagined. Of course, he'd ensured we had the same villa we'd stayed in last year.

My incredible man wrapped his arms around me from behind. Neither one of us spoke for several minutes; we simply stared out across the water from our private balcony, allowing the serenity to blanket us in a bubble of bliss.

"Is this really happening?" I asked, lifting my hand to gaze at the beautiful diamond gracing my wedding finger and sparkling in the moonlight.

Ryan kissed my neck tenderly while his embrace tightened around me. "This is really happening, Holly." The love and certainty in his voice were unmistakeable. "I want you to be officially mine as soon as possible."

Turning in his arms, I gazed up into his eyes. "I am officially yours and you're mine, baby. We don't need a piece of paper to prove that."

He kissed my lips hungrily, and his erection pressed hard

against me. "I know, but you're still going to be my wife, and I'll spend the rest of my life trying to be the husband you deserve."

His words turned my brain to mush. "God, I love you, Ryan Davenport."

Placing his hands on my cheeks and a brief kiss on my lips, he replied, "I love you, too, sexy fiancée."

Before I had a chance to decide how I felt about that word, two strong arms scooped me up and carried me back inside. I squealed as I fell to the bed.

"You've got too many clothes on," Ryan said, standing with his arms crossed over his broad chest.

Scuttling backwards, I came to rest against the stack of soft pillows. As I undid the top button of my shirt, I raised my eyebrows. "So do you."

"You first." His demanding tone did wild and wonderful things to my body. I tore through the rest of the buttons and let the shirt fall off my shoulders. Ryan's eyes followed my hands as they reached for the fly of my jeans.

"Enjoying the strip show?" I asked, raising my eyebrows.

Without meeting my gaze, he nodded. "Very much."

His hungry eyes darkened with lust, devouring every inch of me. I felt incredibly sexy and desired.

As seductively as I could manage, I removed the rest of my clothes so I lay in front of the man I never dared dream for completely bare and exposed.

Ryan stripped in a blur of scattered material, and my heart rate sped up as the bed dipped with his weight. He crawled towards me on all fours. I succumbed to his power, his love, and the knowledge that hours earlier he'd asked me to be his forever.

Chapter Thirty-Seven

Six months later

"Good morning, fiancée."

I smiled at the handsome man hovering over me, naked and clearly ready to make it a *very* good morning.

"Good morning, fiancé." It was the way we'd greeted each other every morning for almost six months since getting engaged. I'd stopped worrying about morning breath a while ago, when he'd insisted nothing about me could ever turn him off.

He pushed inside me and kissed me with passion that seemed to grow more with every passing day. I couldn't believe I'd be waking up with this gorgeous man every morning for the rest of my life. I never allowed myself to think it was too good to be true.

"I love you." His words came out in grunts as his thrusts got harder and faster. "When will you be my wife?" This was the same question he asked me every morning, and I never gave him a solid answer.

He knew just how to drive me crazy with lust and ensured I

got my release before he let go himself. Both fully sated, he pulled out slowly and lay on his back next to me, holding my hand. After several minutes of heavy breathing and coming down from our post-orgasmic high, I turned my head to look at Ryan. His smug grin made me chuckle. Sex always made him happy, but then again, Ryan Davenport was all man.

He met my eyes and whispered, "Merry Christmas, Holly."

"Was that my present?" My grin matched his.

"No. I've got something for you." His sapphire eyes lit up with his cheeky grin. "That was mine."

"Oh well. I'll just take your other present back then."

He propped himself up on his elbow. "Depends what it is."

"Let me guess." I propped myself up, too, so I could look directly at him. "Lingerie for me that you can remove anytime you want you'd like to keep?"

"That's why we're meant to be, babe." He raised his eyebrows and tapped the side of his head. "You can read my mind."

I laughed. "You're not that hard to work out."

"Seriously, Holly. I have everything I need right here in this bed. I don't need anything else."

"Bad luck. I got you something anyway." I rolled over to my bedside table and opened the top drawer, pulling out a red box. Ryan was right behind me, kissing the back of my neck. "Hey. You have to open your present first." My heart rate increased when I thought about the past few months of planning that had gone into this.

Ryan groaned, clearly ready for round two. I handed him the box, and he frowned. "You really didn't have to get me anything."

"I know, but I hope you'll like this."

The smile he gave me was filled with such love, I thought my heart might burst. He slowly opened the box, looked inside and his smile disappeared. *He didn't like what he'd found.*

"Really?" His shocked expression was filled with hope as he held up the card I'd placed on top of the gift. He held it up and read the words out loud. "Will you marry me today? I love you."

I nodded and bit my bottom lip. "Surprise?"

"Babe, I've wanted to marry you every day since you said yes, but how can we get married today?" He looked at me with questioning eyes. "It's Christmas."

"It was something my father said a few months ago, actually, and the surprise is a little payback." I thought back to the way Ryan had proposed to me on my birthday at the Hummingbird—the place our relationship had started. Ryan had wanted to give me a reason to be happy again on my birthday when, for the past decade, it hadn't been a day for celebration at all. Instead, it had just been the anniversary of my mother's death.

"What did your father say?"

"He asked what our plans were for Christmas this year, and when I said we hadn't talked about it yet, we started reminiscing about Mum and how crazy she went with decorations, etcetera."

"God, I wish I could've met that woman."

I smiled sadly. "Me too." I shook my head in an effort to dust off the sadness of what I planned to be the happiest day of my life.

He glanced down at the box again and pulled out the photo frame. "Who took this photo?"

"Audrey. She was determined to capture the moment when you dropped to one knee apparently and had her fancy camera ready to go."

Ryan smiled. "That doesn't surprise me." Placing the frame on the bed, he leaned towards me. "So you and your dad were talking about your mother's love of Christmas."

"Yes. So, Dad mentioned he feels her presence strongest at Christmas and always hopes to honour her memory by making Christmas an extra-happy celebration. My first thought on how to do that was marrying you."

"That makes me so insanely happy." He kissed me, and I smiled against his lips. He pulled back. "Tell me everything."

"Dad and Sophie went for the idea straight away, of course, as did April and Jamie. Your mum and Jonathan were over the moon, too. Your dad is coming out of rehab for the day but obviously won't be drinking."

"Bloody hell. You've been busy."

"I've had a lot of willing helpers. Your mum, Sophie, Audrey, Zara, Aspen, Jase and my sisters have all been amazing."

"I am so on board with this, Holly."

I knew he would be even more on board with the fact that he didn't have to be involved in the wedding preparations. "It's nothing extravagant. Just our immediate families and closest friends for the ceremony and lunch at Balmoral Beach."

Ryan shook his head, a look of amazement falling across his gorgeous face. "That sounds so bloody perfect." He pulled me into a hug and kissed my head.

"It does? Are you sure?" I pulled back so I could look in his beautiful eyes.

"I've never been so sure about anything in my entire life," he replied, choked with emotion.

Tears streamed down my face, and I knew this was absolutely going to be the happiest day of our lives.

Chapter Thirty-Eight

Once Ryan had left for his mum's house, I drove to Dad and Sophie's Balmoral apartment to get ready with the girls.

"It's your wedding day," Audrey, Zara, Jamie, and April said in unison the second I walked through the door, followed by high-pitched squeals and a group tackle-hug.

"How are you feeling?" Sophie asked, handing me a flute of champagne and orange juice.

I accepted the bubbles. "I'm ready to do this."

Dad walked in from the kitchen with an enormous smile on his face. "Hello, sweetheart."

The second he spoke, tears blurred my vision. Despite being surrounded by my family, both blood and chosen, I wanted my mother. Perhaps that feeling would never go away and I'd never get accustomed to the loss, but I felt it acutely in that moment. Sensing my mixed emotions, Dad enveloped me in his arms, holding me close so he could whisper in my ear, "She's here with you, Holly. She's with all of us, and she's so proud."

The tears spilled down my cheeks, and I sobbed into his chest. "I'm sorry, Dad."

After a few moments of simply holding me, he pulled back and held me at arm's length. "You needed to let that out now. It's your big day and it's completely natural to wish your mother was here, but this is going to be the happiest day of your life. I know it was for me."

I glanced around, fearful I'd made everyone uncomfortable, especially Sophie, with my emotional outburst, but they'd all left the room, allowing me the space I needed with my dad. I smiled. The lump in my throat had disappeared. "Better now than when I'm saying my vows, right?"

"Absolutely. When you were a little girl, you cried all the time. You weren't a cry baby. It was just your way of venting your emotions so you could get on with it." He swiped the tears from my cheeks with his thumbs, then handed me a tissue he pulled from his pocket. "It's healthy to let it out, Holly. I think we've both learned that in the last year, and my only regret is not helping you grieve your mum in the way I should've known you needed to back then. Instead, I allowed my own grief to cloud everything."

Blowing my nose, I nodded. "No more sad tears today. Deal?"

His eyes lit up. "Deal. Now I think you have a white dress and some ladies waiting for you in the spare bedroom with all manner of hairbrushes and girly stuff."

Smiling, I hugged him again. "Thanks, Dad. I might not have Mum here, but I have you, and I'm so happy you found Sophie. She's a keeper."

When I walked into the spare room, the first thing I saw was the stunning dress, splayed out across the bed. The late-morning sunshine streamed in through the window, casting rays of light across the silk and lace. "It's so beautiful," I crooned, closing the distance to the bed and stroking my fingers gently across the skirt. Turning to find April, I grinned. "Thank you so much. You're extremely talented."

April was studying fashion design at a prestigious Sydney academy and was an insanely talented seamstress. She was the only choice to do the alterations on Mum's wedding dress to make it perfect for me. My first reaction had been horror when Dad, April and Jamie had tabled the idea. We couldn't possibly alter something so precious. When I agreed, it was on the condition that April and Jamie would make their own alterations if they wanted to wear it on their wedding days. Gazing at the dress now, I couldn't imagine wearing anything else and loved the idea of it being such an integral part of all our special days. It was another way of keeping Mum close.

"You're welcome, Hol," April said, beaming with pride. "I can't wait to see it on you with your hair and makeup done. You're going to be the most beautiful bride ever."

"Thanks, gorgeous."

"Okay, Holly," Audrey said. "Go to the bathroom and change. You'll find your sexy underwear and a robe in there. Then get your butt back in this chair." She pointed to the chair by the window.

For the next hour, I was completely at Audrey and Zara's mercy. My only requests had been that my hair be left down and my makeup not be too over-the-top. I knew they wouldn't turn me into a clown, but I also knew they could both get carried away when they were excited.

"It's time to put the dress on," Jamie said, tapping her watch.

"Okay. We're done here," Audrey said, brushing one final stroke over my cheekbone. "You are perfection, Mrs Soon-to-Be Davenport."

"Thank you." I grabbed Audrey and Zara's hands and squeezed them. "I really appreciate all you're doing today. I know it's a family day you're giving up for me."

They both shook their heads, smiling.

"You're family, babe," Zara said. "We wouldn't want to be anywhere else."

"Absolutely," Audrey said. "We love you, and we're not giving anything up. I've never been happier, and I know Anna would be, too."

Hugging them both, and being careful to avoid ruining the hair and makeup I had yet to see, I took in a deep breath, walked over to the bed, and removed my robe. Staring at the beautiful, white dress laid out before me, I wondered if my mum had felt the same way when she'd gone to put it on more than twenty-five years ago. Had she felt the butterflies flapping their wings wildly in her tummy? Had she wanted to both throw up and jump for joy? Had she marvelled at how she'd gotten so lucky to be marrying her best friend and the love of her life? Something deep inside me knew the answer was yes to all those questions. The realisation that I felt connected to her, not just by the dress but by the knowledge that her blood ran in my veins and that she would live on in me, gave me so much peace.

With the girls' help, I stepped into my expertly-altered gown, thrilled by how perfectly it moulded to my body as April zipped it up.

"Oh my God, Hol," Audrey said, her hands covering her mouth and tears glazing her eyes. "You look incredible."

"Hold on a moment," April said, fussing around me. "I still need to tie the sash at the back."

It had been her idea to add a pale yellow, satin sash from another of Mum's dresses Dad had kept. When Mum had died, he'd donated most of her clothes to charity but kept a handful of favourites packed away in a storage container. He'd said he didn't think he'd want to see us wearing the dresses as they were, but loved the idea of them being made into something new and significant.

"Okay," April said, tapping me on the backside. "You're ready."

I smoothed my hands down over my hips and walked to the full-length mirror set up in the corner. When I saw my reflection, I gasped, almost not recognising myself. "Wow."

The girls chuckled. "Wow is the understatement of the century," Audrey said.

The bodice moulded to my curves, then fell to the floor beneath the sash. Intricate lace overlayed the entire dress. It was understated, yet I'd never felt more beautiful and ready to marry Ryan. He told me I was the most beautiful woman in the world every single day, but I was confident he'd be impressed with the results of the girls' handiwork.

Dad rapped his knuckles on the partly-open door. "Knock, knock."

"Come in, Dad." I called out to him, knowing he'd be waiting to make sure I was decent. "I'm almost ready."

When he walked in, I turned to face him, holding my hands

against my stomach to settle my nerves. His eyes widened and his mouth kept opening and closing, but no words came out. I had no idea what he was thinking.

"Is this too hard?" I asked, my shoulders tensing. The dress, despite the alterations, was largely unchanged. I knew I didn't look exactly like her with my much darker hair and slightly smaller frame, but the resemblance was still there. Perhaps this was excruciating for him.

Dad shook his head, then closed the distance, stopping right in front of me. "You look absolutely beautiful, sweetheart. Seeing you in this dress... I admit it took me back when I first saw you, but it makes my heart so happy. Thank you."

Fighting back the emotion and relief, I refused to cry, despite the lump in my throat. "Thanks, Dad. It feels right."

Audrey cleared her throat. "Sophie just called and said everything is set. Ryan is there with his groomsmen." She grinned. "Apparently, he arrived early. Eager much?"

Audrey, Zara, April, and Jamie had managed to get themselves dressed and spruced in record time, wearing simple bridesmaid dresses in the same colour as my sash. I'd let them choose whatever they wanted, and it had been their unanimous decision to honour Mum.

Dad crooked his elbow. "Let's go get you married."

"You don't have to sound quite so enthusiastic, Dad," I said, feigning hurt.

His shoulders shook with laughter. "I'm kidding!"

It was music to my ears and heart hearing him so light-hearted and happy.

April handed me my flowers - a stunning arrangement of

white roses and jasmine. Lifting it to my nose, I inhaled the beautiful scent. I'd never been more ready to make this lifelong commitment, despite the risks of life and love.

***

The wedding guests were small in number, but Ryan and I knew everyone in attendance. I never wanted to be introduced to anyone at my own wedding. I was confident Ryan would be more than happy with a small, intimate gathering, and there was no way I'd wanted an extravaganza. By the time Dad and I crossed the small stone bridge leading from the beach to the headland where the ceremony would take place, anxiety took a stranglehold on my throat.

"Hey. Easy on the death grip," Dad said, patting my hand that dug into his forearm. "Just relax. Everything is precisely as it's supposed to be. You can't control anything but the here and now."

Calm descended over me like a blanket, and I relaxed my grip. He'd said exactly what I needed to hear at that moment, as if he had some kind of father–daughter intuition. "Sorry, Dad. I just had a brief freak-out, but I'm fine."

We continued our walk up the gentle slope. When we reached the highest point, we could see the wedding guests waiting for us just down the other side, close to the southern edge of the headland. The melodic sound of the string quartet intermingled with the hum of activity all around us. I knew I'd only have a few moments before someone noticed us, so I took the opportunity to soak in the sight. Jonathan had his arm around Jessica's shoulders – a perfect picture of love being found in second chances. Ryan's father, Daniel, was talking to Jason and Aspen. I believed he would respect our day and be on his best behaviour. Audrey and Zara were lined up facing the guests with Sydney Harbour as their backdrop. It was simply stunning. Sophie stood next to them, smiling as she chatted to April and Jamie. I loved that they had such a good relationship. Dressed in an elegant, soft pink shift dress, she was our marriage celebrant. It was one of the reasons I could set my wedding day today. Not many celebrants worked on Christmas.

Glancing to the left of Sophie, my breath caught. Ryan had seen me and was looking directly into my soul with searing lust and lasting love. I'd been insanely attracted to him from the moment I first saw him in the café, and that attraction grew stronger every day. As I looked back at my man, I saw everything I wanted for my future. I saw *him*. For a day, a year, a decade, or ideally until we were both old and grey, I wanted him by my side.

The guests turned their heads. This was officially happening. I tugged on Dad's arm. "Let's get down there so I can get myself married."

"Now who's the enthusiastic one?" he asked, nudging me in the side.

"Yeah, yeah. Let's go."

The guests stood and made an aisle. With my father by my side, I made my final walk as a single woman amongst all the people I loved and cherished. I accepted whispered compliments with a grateful smile. When we reached the front, I brimmed with happiness as Dad shook Ryan's hand, kissed me on the cheek, then stepped back into the front row of guests.

Ryan, it seemed, couldn't take his eyes off me, and when I stepped in front of him, he leaned forward and kissed me, then whispered against my lips, "You're breathtaking."

Sophie cleared her throat, to the amusement of the guests. Ryan and I took a step back sheepishly.

The next thirty minutes were a blur of easily-made promises and legal obligations. I think we were both waiting for the 'I now pronounce you husband and wife' and 'you may kiss the bride'. When they finally came, Ryan crashed his lips to mine.

It was official, it felt fantastic and part of me wanted to skip straight to tonight when we'd be alone and naked. Pushing those thoughts away, given it was Christmas and our guests were here just for us, I squeezed Ryan's hand. Together, we turned to face our family and friends as man and wife.

Chapter Thirty-Nine

Perhaps if we'd had our wedding day at a different time of year, we might've had our reception at the iconic Bathers' Pavilion, overlooking Balmoral Beach. Apparently, the dining room walls were covered with twelve hundred sheets of silver to mimic the light on the water, seen through the unique box windows. But we were married on Christmas Day, and we were going to have a seafood barbeque on the beach in true Aussie style. We had gained permission to set up tables and chairs on the beachside gardens. As there were only twenty guests, we didn't take up too much space.

After we'd eaten our fill of garlic-drenched lobster and marinated prawns, Ryan stood, lifting the microphone to his mouth. I drank in the supreme handsomeness of the man I could now call my husband.

He cleared his throat, then began. "I think I can speak on behalf of my wife when I thank you so much for being here for the best day of our lives. Without a doubt, I'm the luckiest bastard to ever walk the face of this earth to say this beautiful woman beside me agreed to be mine." He shook his head as if he didn't quite believe his own words. Taking a deep breath, he turned to face me. "Holly, my wife." He chuckled. "I think I'm going to have to keep saying that until it truly sinks in."

I winked at him.

He continued. "Babe, I would've married you at a registry office with no one else there. I would've eloped with you to a Vegas chapel and said my vows in front of Elvis, or I would've committed my life to you at St Mary's Cathedral in front of a million people." His eyes went glassy as the emotion seemed to overwhelm him for a moment. "I didn't care where or how, to be perfectly honest, but on a Sydney beach with our family and friends, on a day when you feel your mum would be happiest …" He reached for my hand and squeezed. "It just feels right." Tears welled in my eyes. I didn't think I could love this man any more than I did, but I was wrong. My heart simply expanded.

"George," Ryan said, directing his gaze to my father. "Thank you for giving me your blessing to marry your daughter." My father nodded, then smiled at me as Ryan continued, "You taught us that what Holly and I have is worth the risk. None of us know what the future holds. Every single day I share with the love of my life will be treasured, and I'll never take a second of it for granted." He met my gaze. "I love you so much, Holly Davenport."

A tear slipped down my cheek. I was losing the battle to keep them at bay. How on earth was I going to speak after him? "I love you," I said, determined to hold myself together for a little longer at least.

Ryan leaned down and kissed me lightly before addressing our guests again. "And because I'm a traditional guy, I believe it's time for me to make a toast." He picked up his glass of champagne and held it in front of him. "Please raise a glass to Holly's bridesmaids, Audrey and Zara, who've been her rocks for far longer than I've known her." He raised his glass higher. "To the bridesmaids."

We all repeated his toast, taking sips of champagne. I locked eyes with my two best friends. Audrey was teary, of course, and Zara beamed with happiness. I blew them kisses.

After thanking my husband, I took the microphone, then pushed my shoulders back to steel myself. I'd had time to prepare a speech and wanted to deliver the words I meant from the bottom of my heart without choking on tears.

Glancing around the room, I withered. I didn't like the limelight, and every set of eyes were zeroed in on me. *Breathe in, breathe out, Holly.*

"Obviously, I couldn't have pulled off today without all of your help. Ryan might've blindsided me with his proposal, but I think I may have just one-upped him."

Everyone snickered, including Ryan. "Don't get used to it," he whispered.

"Anyway," I continued, smiling. "As most of you know, the reason I wanted to do this on Christmas Day was for my mum, who sadly isn't with us anymore." I glanced at Dad, and he gave me an encouraging smile. "She loved the decorations that appeared in shops months in advance. She loved the pop-up shops, the scout halls selling real fir trees, and she loved eggnog." I smiled, remembering how her eyes lit up when she saw someone attaching lights to their roofline. "But more than any of these things, she loved the family time, and she would've loved to have been here today, watching me marry the love of my life, surrounded by family and friends." I paused, glancing at the smiling faces. "I know it's everything she would've ever wanted for her children, so having it on her favourite day of the year is my way of saying thank you." I choked back tears as I felt her presence wrap around me. I looked up to the deep blue sky scattered with wispy clouds. "Mum, I wish you were here. I wish you'd met Ryan." I glanced at my husband. "You would've loved him."

Ryan stood up and put his arm around my shoulders, kissing the top of my head and giving me the strength to continue.

"I wish she was here to share today with me, and I know there'll be more milestones ahead that she'll miss." Allowing a tear to fall down my cheek, I shook my head. "But I've learnt in this past year, thanks to all of you here today, that living every day to the fullest and embracing love, if you're lucky enough to come across it, is what life's all about. I'll never fear the 'what ifs' again because I have so much love in my life and my heart to overcome anything, and what an incredible gift that is." I swiped the tears from my cheeks and raised my glass. "To chance encounters, love and happily ever afters. Merry Christmas, Mum."

All the people I loved in the world stood up, raising their glasses, and cheered. "Merry Christmas!"

By late afternoon, the last of our guests had left, and Ryan and I caught a taxi home. I saw no reason to hire a fancy car to take us fifteen minutes away. Of course, when we arrived at our apartment door, Ryan scooped me into his arms to carry me across the threshold. It was completely old-fashioned given we already lived together, but I loved it all the same.

"Do you feel any different?" he asked, setting me down in front of the floor-to-ceiling glass overlooking the Harbour Bridge, keeping his arms around me.

I nodded. "I do."

"They're my favourite words."

"I do?"

He chuckled. "When you said it during the ceremony, I almost let out a loud whoop."

"Why didn't you?"

"I didn't want to appear relieved that my fiancée would actually go through with marrying me. I had to maintain some dignity."

I ran my fingers down his shirt, popping the buttons as I went. "Did you really think I wouldn't go through with it?"

He planted his hands on top of mine, stopping my progress. "I know you love me, Holly, and I know you wanted this, but I still see fear in your eyes." One of his hands left mine and cupped my cheek. "These beautiful eyes don't lie, and I know there might always be a small part of you that fears what happened to your mum will happen to you. I know you fear what that would do to me."

My heart stopped for a beat. "Why would you say this to me now? We're married. I *married* you. I rose above those fears."

"I love every part of you with all that I am and all that I'll ever be." Now both his hands cupped my cheeks. "I need you to know that you never need to hide that fear and pretend it's completely gone away. There are no guarantees in life, and no one can tell you, me, or anyone that nothing bad is going to happen, but we're in this together, come what may."

He had ripped out my heart but then held it in his hands with such absolute reverence so it could beat stronger than ever before. Knowing he understood that part of me and accepted it felt like a tiny missing piece to my puzzle had been slotted in. Ryan completed me in every way.

"Come what may," I repeated.

"Forever and always."

THE END

Also by Kate Sterritt

The Fight for Life Series (Romantic suspense)
Collision (Book 1)
Impact (Book 2)

Standalone Novel
Love My Way (Contemporary Romance/ Women's Fiction)

About the Author

Kate Sterritt lives in Sydney, Australia with her husband, three young sons and highly energetic German Shorthaired Pointer puppy. When she's not madly juggling the logistics of soccer trainings, play dates and volunteering at the school, she can be found at her laptop, writing the types of novels she loves to read. Her characters are inspired by her own experiences, blended with her imagination and a healthy dose of wishful thinking.

Connect with Kate
www.katesterritt.com
Facebook.com/authorkatesterritt
Twitter.com/KASterritt
Instagram.com/katesterritt
kasterritt@gmail.com
Facebook readers group Kate Sterritt's Hummingbirds

"Legends say that hummingbirds float free of time, carrying our hopes for love, joy and celebration. Hummingbirds open our eyes to the wonder of the world and inspire us to open our hearts to loved ones and friends. Like a hummingbird, we aspire to hover and to savor each moment as it passes, embrace all that life has to offer and to celebrate the joy of everyday. The hummingbird's delicate grace reminds us that life is rich, beauty is everywhere, every personal connection has meaning and that laughter is life's sweetest creation." – PAPYRUS

Acknowledgements

To my dad. Thank you for loving Mum with an unwavering fierceness that inspired this story, for always picking me up on my grammar and for teaching me the joy of finding spelling mistakes in restaurant menus.

To my husband and our three sons. My heart grows bigger every day because of you.

To my sisters and friends, here and around the world. Thank you for your love, support and encouragement. Many of you became a very special part of my writing journey. I am blessed to have you in my life.

Thank you also to Lucy Fenton and Kristin Albright, my two author friends who were always willing to share their own writing and publishing experiences. I really appreciated it.

And finally, a special mention to my friend, GJ Walker-Smith. Your writing inspires me. Your guidance and friendship have changed my life. Thank you for all your help and for giving me the confidence to pursue this dream.

www.ingramcontent.com/pod-product-compliance
Lightning Source LLC
Chambersburg PA
CBHW050026180626
46810CB00002B/591